SARAH JANE HUNTINGTON

VELOX BOOKS
Published by arrangement with the author.

CONTENTS

Introduction _____ 1

Deja Vu _____ 4

Stranger in a Known Land _____ 13

A Tourists Guide to the Galaxy _____ 24

Written on a Subway Wall _____ 35

Search For Answers _____ 54

Mirror Darkly _____ 67

Holes _____ 78

A Most Curious Collection _____ 94

Such a Perfect Day _____ 111

Trapped _____ 121

Exploration For Humanity _____ 140

Will The Real Alexander Please Stand Up _____ 157

The Keeper of the Lake _____ 168

End Notes _____ 178

INTRODUCTION
OR RATHER, ME, RAMBLING ON (FEEL FREE TO SKIP)

Since I was a child, books have been my entire world. In them, I could experience a thousand lives in vast futuristic cities or visit alternate fantasy worlds, battle monsters and make new friends who only belonged on paper.

I could escape bullies and bad situations, and even live the life of someone else, however briefly.

Until one ordinary night, an old black and white episode of *The Twilight Zone* aired. One was all it took before I was hooked.

The episode was 'The Monsters are Due on Maple Street' (Season 1, Episode 22)

There was no happy ending, and the audience was left able to use their own imagination over what might come next. The plot captivated me.

It was a show where the impossible could become quite ordinary.

The extraordinary stories often had no answers, and I loved that aspect because it meant I could think and dream up my own version of what came next.

People from all walks of life had wild run-ins with the unknown. *The Twilight Zone* often taught lessons too and warned of dangerous days ahead. It taught us that there is simply just so much that we do not know.

The impact the show had on countless people is phenomenal. It encompassed everything. Aliens, the occult, space travel, wormholes, science fiction, strange objects, etc.

For me, each one was a masterpiece in its own right.

The moment I heard Rod Serling's delicious voice, my excitement and escape would begin. *The Outer Limits* and *Amazing Stories* were equally as inspiring to many, and of course, *The X-files* and so on.

By the time I had hit my twenties, I had seen every episode several times. I began to write my own. Of course, we are self-critical of ourselves. I fully accepted that I could never hope to write as cleverly or as elegantly as all those episodes were and still are, and nor would I waste my time trying.

I need to make that clear.

Although these stories are inspired by *The Twilight Zone* and other similar shows, I am fully aware that I do not possess the clever mind to write as expertly as all those episodes were written! :)

Instead, I wanted to create something similar, something different. Something simple and fun, maybe even humorous, too.

Plain, simple horror, and unusual stories are what I adore to write. Social commentaries, political statements, intricate worlds, and so on, are not my thing. I enjoy reading stories like that, but not writing them.

I don't believe there always has to be an explanation in a story. I like the idea that a reader can make their own theory.

I decided that maybe someone would read something I wrote and smile. Or better yet, they might remember it and wonder, what if?

I re-read everything I had ever written all those years ago.

Eighty percent needed nothing more than the rubbish bin to and never see the light of day.

The remaining twenty, I began to wonder about. Could I, or should I?

I have never copied (to the best of my knowledge) the plots of *The Twilight Zone*. Rather, I tried to dream up new scenarios, new twists, and fresh ideas. That isn't always possible, of course, almost everything has been done countless times, but that wouldn't stop me from putting my own stamp on something.

The Twilight Zone has inspired me multiple times over. In writing and in life, too.

I don't like limits and I despise rules. I love plot twists, whether predictable or not.

I love ordinary people, experiencing the impossible. Which is not at all impossible, after all.

We place limits on reality, we decide what might be possible and what isn't.

I like to think anything can happen and sometimes, it does.

I decided I did not want these stories to rattle around in my (mostly empty) skull any longer. I did not want them to sit in the depths of an old cupboard collecting dust and nothing more.

I want them to see the light of day and hopefully, be enjoyed. If only one person reads these tales and smiles or wonders, then I have achieved something beyond wonderful. I will have achieved what I always believed was an impossibility.

With all that being said, take a trip with me to realms unknown. To places of wonder where the impossible can occur and does.

Where situations are really not at all what they first seem to be.

Truly, what is our place in the vast universe, and what are we really?

Visit with me, a place some do not return from. The middle ground between light and shadow…

Because truly, *what if?*

DEJA VU

For your consideration. Meet twenty-eight-year-old husband and father of three, Mr. Leon Gregory. An exhausted, resentful soul by all accounts, and one with a most violent temper.

Leon Gregory, a dead man walking. A man who longs for death. A man whose time may be about to be cut short. A man that will do anything, for just a little peace and quiet…

Day One

Leon Gregory wakes with a fierce jolt. His alarm plays its relentless symphony straight down his ear. He is sick of the sound. He feels exhausted. Feverish, achy, and his head is pounding.

Besides him, his wife Lacy stirs and groans.

It's okay for her, he thinks. She gets to stay home while I work hard all day.

Leon and Lacy, Lacy and Leon. The two names flow together in perfect-sounding harmony, a harmony that does not exist within their short marriage.

Leon thinks briefly of the day Lacy told him she was pregnant. At first, he felt pleased and happy, until he realized her religiously minded father meant to force the two to marry.

Three years and three children later, Leon feels more trapped and suffocated than ever.

It does not occur to him that his wife might feel the same.

He hates the smell of Lacy, the scent of cabbage and cheap lavender mixed together. He hates her voice, the high-pitched tones, and the shrillness. Most of all, he hates her face. Loathes looking at her. She is his constant reminder that he is trapped.

He also despises his children, a fact he keeps hidden carefully inside.

He sees chubby arms and legs and greedy mouths to feed. He hears non-stop crying and wailing, seeing only the cost of each one.

He is sick of working six days a week only for his wage to be taken immediately. Every pound is spent on a mortgage he never wanted, food he never gets to eat. Gas and electricity he doesn't get to enjoy.

Leon hates his house. He hates the creaking stairs, the leaking roof, and the expense. He hates the second-hand clothes that hang in his donated wardrobe.

He once had dreams. Grand dreams of traveling and exploring vast new lands.

Leon wants to die.

He wants to put a gun to his head and end it all.

He rises from the cheap bed with its cheap scratchy sheets, dresses quickly, and heads downstairs. Maybe he can leave before the morning chaos? Before the wailing of the children starts, before his wife begins her complaining. He plots his escape.

No time for toast, but there isn't any bread anyway. He swallows a bitter coffee and leaves, shuts the door quietly, and runs across the overgrown lawn.

He hasn't mown the grass in a while. He can't. The machine broke and there isn't enough money to buy a new one or even enough to repair the old one.

Every penny is swallowed up by the house and its human contents. His neighbors have started complaining, Lacy told him. They moan about the state of his house. What can he do? He doesn't have the money.

Leon wishes he could die.

Maybe he could get run over? By a huge heavy goods lorry, something quick and fatal. Or he could swallow poison. Where might he buy poison from? He wouldn't want to suffer. No, he feels he suffers enough already.

He thinks of his options as he walks to work, down the streets he's walked a thousand or more times, straight to the mines that are killing him slowly and without his knowledge.

Down, down into darkness and fear. Pits of black despair. Back-breaking work. Horrible and cruel. Wretched.

"Morning," one of his fellow mine workers says.

Leon snaps out of his daydream and blinks rapidly.

A feeling he can't explain washes over him, a chaotic sensation he doesn't have the right word for. The sense he has lived the exact same moment before.

In a way, he has. Every day except Sunday is a repeat of the day before and the day before that.

Sleep, wake, work, hurt, eat, argue, sleep. The familiar pattern is now ingrained inside his very cells.

"Leon, you okay mate?"

"Yeah," he answers. "I was miles away."

Truly, he wishes he was.

The workers make their way into the pits, plunging down inside a metal cage, huddled in beside several other weary men. Off into the deepest darkness.

No sunlight. Only pitch black. What kind of life is this?

Leon has nothing to look forward to. No holiday time, not like the other men. He cannot recall why he has none, only that he doesn't. He hasn't been anywhere.

He has no days away to lie on a soft, warm beach. No big meal waiting at home, no fresh bread or real meat. They can't afford such extravagances. Only misery beckons. Endless misery.

Repeat, repeat, repeat. Exit all hope.

Even his dreams are empty. Leon feels he closes his eyes for seconds, only to hear his alarm begin.

The cage stops, he is jostled by other men keener to work than he is.

Wearily, already hungry, he steps out. Pain starts as soon as he begins his work. It hurts to breathe, hurts to bend and move. A vicious pain that tears his spine and soul.

There are no other jobs available anywhere. He can't take a day off to go job hunting or attend interviews. Less wages would mean hell for him.

The other men sing happy songs and tell filthy stories to occupy themselves.

"And then she said, course I will, Darling!" A man laughs as he finishes his outrageous tale.

Laughter erupts around him. The sound makes Leon's heart quiver and stutter.

He feels that odd sensation again. He's heard that story before. Was it yesterday or the day before, or both? He can't recall. The sensation makes him feel as if he has insects crawling around inside his skull.

Time passes slowly. Far too slowly.

Leon wants to die.

What kind of life is this?

A silly mistake with a local girl who smells of cabbage and cheap lavender, a marriage he didn't want, three children he didn't want. No money, there is never any money for him. There isn't even enough spare for the newspapers anymore.

He used to love reading the Sunday papers, alone and in peace. Now, he doesn't have a clue about what might be happening in the world.

He misses that peace, his one slice of quiet.

He longs for silence. Just five minutes a day would be nice.

Instead, despair is his companion.

The men around him talk of going to the local pub after work. Leon loves the pub, but he hasn't been for years. He likes to drink ale and stare at the barmaid's chest. He always thought she was a looker. He's willing to bet she wouldn't complain and whine all the time. He wouldn't mind waking up next to her every morning either, but no, he's stuck with cabbage breath and the noisy brats.

He glances at his watch, realizing it's stopped. Now he doesn't know how much time is passing. His stomach rumbles loudly. He feels the quake, the complaint of his insides. He has no pack-up to eat at break. There wasn't enough money to buy extra food. No, his youngest is growing too quickly, he needs new shoes. Lacy insisted.

Seconds drag like hours, minutes feel like days.

He hears the shrill of a whistle.

Break time.

He intends to stand away from the men, or they'll tease him for being poor and having no food. They won't offer him any, they never do. He knows this as fact, but he can't remember how.

He climbs into the cage, back up to the surface world, back to the fresh air.

At least the air is free. That hasn't been taxed yet.

7

Break time drags on and on and on. Nothing ever changes.

Leon wants to die. He wants to die so very much.

Finally, finish time. It's late, he thinks. But there will be some food, even if it's just a little broth and some stale bread at the house. Just like the night before and the night before that.

Leon retraces his steps home, the route he has taken a thousand times or more. The same route with its cracked pavements and broken streetlight.

He is exhausted. Beyond tired.

Still, the children will be asleep at least. He might have half an hour of peace just for himself. What a rare treat that would be.

But the treat would have to end, and that makes having something good all the more unbearable.

His day off, Sunday, feels impossibly far off. As if it might never arrive at all.

Perhaps it won't.

Leon wants to die.

He sees his house, the most untidy one on the street, the dirty one, the poor looking one, and feels a heavy sense of dread and shame.

He opens his front door, belly full of hunger and apprehension. He freezes.

Chaos, noise, and calamity inside. His children, he forgets who is who, run around half-naked and in filthy nappies while the kitchen looks as if a bomb went off.

Hands paw at him, cries of his children deafen him. They clutch at him, wailing like little monsters and covered in paint.

Messy painted handprints trail across the grimy walls.

Hot rage begins to rise.

"Lacy!" He yells. "Where are you?"

He finds his wife outside, talking to a neighbor over the fence, chatting as if she doesn't have a care in the world. Laughing and smiling with the gossip next door.

How dare she, how dare she laugh and enjoy her life?

After all he has to do to keep her and the children fed and a roof over their heads. How dare she feel happy when he can't.

All the hard work, all the endless sacrifices. He never gets his peace and quiet.

"Get inside!" Leon bellows. "Now! The children need you."

Red-faced, caught out, Lacy rushes in. Leon can smell cabbage. Cabbage and decay. Ungratefulness and spite.

The hot rage begins its spiraling, its boiling.

"What did you cook? I'm hungry," Leon seethes. Each word tastes bitter on his tongue. Sour and vile.

The children are screaming, red-faced tantrums. Leon cannot think straight. The sounds only escalate. Louder, louder.

He starts to shake, can feel the quivers of hate begin in his toes and spread.

"I've not had the chance yet. I've been busy," Lacy says. "Besides, there isn't much. Only enough for the kids. You'll have to work extra hours again."

His wife's words echo and bounce somehow, into his ears and around his mind.

Anger boils over until his body jerks.

He knows this feeling well. The mist of rage, of fury.

This is like the time he punched his wife for dropping his best mug, or like the time she told him she was pregnant for the third time. Or when she forgot to pay the gas bill. Or the time she threatened to leave him.

Remember how he begged her, recall how he pleaded and promised to change? No, he should have let her leave. He can't allow this woman to dictate his life anymore.

His brain freezes and fills with a block of ice. His limbs shudder. He snaps, breaks, unable to take the pressure, the stress, the hunger anymore. Vicious hate surfaces. A brutal explosion inside.

Leon does not want to die. He wants his wife to die instead.

His hands reach out and circle her throat, he squeezes hard. His arms are strong from working the pits. She cannot scream, cannot speak. She has no air.

The children squeal for her. Screams of horror burst from their tiny lungs as they watch their mother dying.

Leon can only squeeze harder, harder. Until Lacy's face turns a curious shade of purple. Only then, only when he is sure, does he let her go.

No more cabbage and cheap lavender smell.

She crumples to the ground, folded up on herself. Onto the clean tiles she scrubs every day.

"SHUT UP!" Leon roars.

The children do not.

Leon cannot think.

His hands find a saucepan, the big heavy one they received as a wedding present. He hits each child repeatedly. A vile, brutal attack. Blow after blow until all are still.

Finally, silence. Peace and quiet.

***

The knock at the door, the heavy thudding breaks him from his daze.

"Police," a deep voice calls. "A disturbance was reported."

Leon wonders what they mean. What disturbance?

He looks at the bodies on the kitchen floor, the pools of blood collected around his feet. It is as if he is seeing the scene for the first time. Terror strikes him, pure undiluted terror with madness biting closely at its heels.

He wonders how they all came to be dead, wonders if someone broke in.

Cold shock floods him. He stares at his hands. At his killer's hands. He did it and he knows it. He murdered them all.

He jerks wildly and vomits down his clothes.

No, no, what have I done?! NO! My family!

The thudding at the door comes louder, the noise of smashed glass and chaos.

Big men push him to the ground as saliva drips down his face.

"I... I... didn't..."

Leon tries to tell them that he didn't mean it. He only lost his temper, that's all. He's fine again now. How can they all be dead? He only wanted some peace.

Shock floods his system. Shame and disgust.

He understands he will go to prison for a very long time. A small part of Leon, a part he doesn't dare to acknowledge, feels grateful he will have regular food and quiet.

In handcuffs, thrown in a cell, Leon cries loudly. Truly, he hadn't meant to hurt anyone. He loved his children. Didn't he? He loved his cabbage-scented wife... once, anyway.

Horror makes way for comprehension. He is evil. He has done a very bad thing. He looks around his cell at the walls he feels sure he's seen before. At the hard stone ground he is certain he has stared at many times over.

It is all too familiar. The strangeness frightens Leon. The clarity of repeat, of living the moment before.

Somehow, he knows what happens next.

A sharp pain bursts across his chest. He gasps for breath. He can't get the air he needs, the air that is supposed to be free.

Another pain, a dull ache in his left arm. His head lolls forward before it snaps back.

I'm dying.

Brutal pain now, his heart thuds and struggles loudly. Beat, beat, stop.

Leon falls forward, a rag doll of a man. His skull cracks on the hard floor. Still, he can't feel it. Leon wished he was dead and now he is.

***

All he sees is darkness, blackness. The absence of all light. A sudden understanding hits him. He is dead, but not. Finished, but still aware.

Knowledge floods. He is a killer, a murderer of the innocent. A stealer of life. There is a special place for him, a special layer. Tucked away somewhere in the place that comes after life is over.

Leon feels as if he is being pulled apart. Wrenched apart inside by invisible hands with sharp, vicious, hot claws.

His wife and children are someplace else, someplace good. He senses that and understands he is not. He is in Hell, or some tangled, warped version of. Set on repeat. The same vicious day over and over. One endless day. Repeat, repeat, repeat.

Leon wants to truly die, to cease to exist. He cannot.

He is condemned, he is punished, for eternity.

No escape. Exit all hope.

Day One

Leon Gregory wakes with a fierce jolt. His alarm plays its relentless symphony straight down his ear. He is sick of the sound. He feels exhausted. Feverish, achy, and his head is pounding.

11

Besides him, his wife Lacy stirs and groans…

Leon Gregory, a bitter man with a most vicious temper. Condemned to live the same dreadful day of his life on an endless loop. Not for a short time, not for a long time, but for infinity.

Somewhere, beyond time and space, beyond dimensions of wonder, lies a realm created purely for the wicked, for the damned. Constructed from cruelty and chaos, inhabited only by the most ruthless of killers.

A special place of Hell indeed…

STRANGER IN A KNOWN LAND

Witness Mr. Tom Pritchard. Age, a young, and perhaps naïve, twenty-three.

Occupation: Fisherman.

A kind man, a devout and simple man, a husband, and soon-to-be first-time father. He is about to take a peculiar journey into realms quite uncharted, a realm he might never return from. A realm beyond his, and maybe our own, understanding.

A singular journey into time and space, new dimensions, and strange yet familiar lands.

Destination: Quite unknown…

Tom Pritchard did not see the storm approach. The sky was blue, and then it was not.

The curious suddenness of the weather made him shiver with nerves and apprehension. Quietly, he hauled up the fishing nets and warned the handful of men who worked alongside him on the small fishing trawler.

The forecast hadn't given out storm warnings, and the one drawing near looked to be fairly severe. He knew the vast seas often had a mind of their own. Still, the strange dark cloud had formed far too swiftly for his liking. Why, it was almost sinister.

While the almost black cloud hovered menacingly over the sea, inside the cloud, Tom could see flashes of blue and white. Lightning, he supposed.

Sometimes, it seemed, the ocean wanted to keep its fishy treasures hidden under the cold surface for itself.

Bad weather was commonplace, but Tom had never seen such a strange storm before, had never even heard of one appearing so quickly.

"Come on Lad," the man that was both his captain and Father spoke. "Get inside, tis' a bad one this."

Tom nodded and felt the stirrings of fear. That look on his father's face made his stomach cramp painfully.

Of course, he'd been in rough seas and terrible weather before, days when the ocean pounded against the trawler and tried its best to shake the boat clean off its surface.

The men gathered inside the wheelhouse as the first heavy rain began to fall. Tom could sense static, electricity in the air. The rain itself felt more like hail. Sharp little daggers falling from the stern darkness.

"We'll be fine," Tom said out loud, more to persuade himself than the others. He shut the outer door firmly as if a thin piece of wood might keep out such terror.

The men clustered by the window to watch.

Tom was willing to bet they all wished they were anywhere else but inside the boat, in the small pub perhaps, drinking ale by a warm fire, or curled up with their soft-skinned wives.

He wished he were safe and sound with his own wife, Heather. If she saw the storm from the village, he knew she'd be worried sick about him.

"Strangest weather I ever saw," one of the men grumbled. The tone of his voice was filled with anxiety.

Tom looked at his father, trying to read his expression. He turned the boat's wheel and remained grim-faced.

Tom peered between men, trying to get a fresh look at the chaos bearing down. The storm had formed itself into a tight, angry ball, almost a perfect sphere. It was barreling towards them as if it had the trawler as its set destination in mind.

Tendrils of lightning flicked out from around the sphere, white and blue sparks escaped and lashed out angrily.

The boat began its undulation, rocking treacherously from side to side. Tom immediately felt sick.

"Change course!" A man yelled.

They could hear the vicious roar of the sea pounding at their ears and boat. The ocean screamed in protest and rage.

14

"Already did, damn thing keeps headin' our way!" The captain shouted.

Tom stepped back, away from the window, back, back until his spine pressed against the wall.

Something was wrong, he could feel it, although he couldn't say what invoked such emotion inside him.

The men, all older than him, turned. He saw faces filled with fear and dread. Mouths moved but he couldn't hear the words. They were telling him to do something, but he didn't understand what it was he should be doing.

The sound of rushing waves, of fierce seas, felt relentless.

Arms reached out to grab surfaces. One glimpse at his father saw him battling the wheel. A battle he seemed to be losing.

Were they going to sink? Were they going to die? Their situation had happened too quickly, with not enough time to think or plan. Tom wasn't ready, wasn't ready to die and drown. No one ever was.

As the men dropped to lay on the wooden floor, Tom stood frozen. In his mind, he prayed. Pressure rose, a feeling as if he was being squashed from the inside.

Though I walk through the valley of the shadow of...

Smash. BOOM.

The storm hit with all the force of a tornado, a wild rush of fierce screaming wind. Thick windows burst apart. He fell, knocked, and was easily beaten by the mighty storm. The last image in his mind was of his wife, his beautiful pregnant wife, before blackness claimed him.

***

Calmness. Quiet.

The gentle bobbling of the boat on still, gentle water.

Tom licked his cracked lips and found he could taste salt. His body felt sore, battered.

Was it all a dream? Am I in bed, safe?

His hands reached out and explored.

No, not in bed. Lying on a cold, wet, wooden floor. Carefully, he cracked open one eye and stared around him. Glass, thousands of shattered pieces surrounded him, all sparkling, caught in the bright sunlight. He blinked rapidly and tried to sit up.

That storm! That awful storm.

The trawler was in one piece. A miracle, he assumed. God had seen their fear, heard their prayer, and took pity. Or maybe it was great Poseidon himself who had assisted the men.

"Father?" He croaked. No one. Where were the men? Surely not overboard?

Tom scrambled up in a panic.

Where was everyone? Assessing the damage? Why hadn't they thought to help him?

Quickly, he stood, his head pounding with pain. Blood dripped in a single line from his nose. He wiped it on his sleeve and yanked at the door. The door itself gave him a fight, warped by water and what else? He braced his foot against the frame and pulled it open, and ran out onto the deck.

"Hello?" He called. No one. No trace of anyone. "Where are you all? Father?"

Silence. Only impossibly loud silence.

Overhead, an army of seagulls arrived and began to swoop and dive.

He stumbled to the port side and peered over. The water looked perfect, still and calm. No men overboard. But fishes, hundreds of dead fishes, floated on the surface, eyes, and mouths wide open.

He squinted, saw the trawler had been swept close to the shoreline, close to his village, his home. A small boat was coming towards him, with two or maybe three men rowing.

Rescue, but where are they all? Did they get swept away to the shore? Is Father alive?

Tom waved his arms frantically, unsure of what to do. Should he jump into the water and search, or were they dead, taken by the ocean they each loved so dearly?

Tom held his head in his hands and cried, cursing himself. It wouldn't do to be so upset when the boat came. He was a fisherman, after all, and fishermen were meant to be brave.

"Ahoy!" Tom heard. He knew the voice, a friend of his father's, Alan.

"I can't find them," Tom babbled as the boat pulled up next to his own. "There was a storm and now they've gone."

"Who's gone?" Alan said as he tied a rope in a complicated knot and attached the two boats together.

"All of them, even my father. I don't know what to do."

"Calm down. Musta bin a mighty big ole storm to finish all these fishes off."

"It was, but the men, my father, please."

"Listen, let's get ya' back to the shore and ya' can tell us who ya' lost. Might be that they washed up just fine. Where ya' come from?"

What?

Tom wiped his face, believing he must be covered in wounds or blood and unrecognizable. Still, Alan should know the boat. He helped his father build it three years back.

"It's me, Tom," Tom assured him.

"Well, nice to meet ya, Tom. Now, back to shore, you'll be needing someone to look at those injuries I reckon."

"Alan, I know you! It's me. Tom Pritchard."

"Don't know any Pritchards, might be that ya' clobbered ya' head Lad."

Confusion and fear rose inside him. His vision swam, an invasion of black spots engulfed his sight. A second storm started up inside his head.

What's happening? I don't understand? It's Alan, he knows me!

The confusion felt too much for his mind to handle. Worry and fear squeezed his skull until sparks of pain flashed. For the second time that day, Tom hit the floor.

***

He woke up and felt softness underneath him. A mattress, warm and dry.

Was it all a dream, just a nightmare?

He opened his eyes and jolted up, his mind spiraled in horror. No, it hadn't been a nightmare at all.

He was in a bed, in an unfamiliar room. Paintings of ships and wild oceans decorated the walls. A small single chair sat in one corner.

He fought off dizziness as he stood, stopping briefly to sit down when the threat of blacking out struck him. Hunger made his stomach growl, but there was no time for food. He had to find the men, and find Heather. A mirror caught his eye, a plain old mirror hanging by the door. Tom peered warily at himself. Yes, he had a few cuts and bruises, but he looked the same as he always had.

"Hello?" He called as he opened the bedroom door. Wait, he knew the house. He was in Alan's home.

Why wasn't he at his own home with Heather? Was she in labor? Had they found the men washed up ashore?

Thought after thought, question after question tumbled around in his mind. He wandered through the house, looking for signs of life. No one.

He felt thoroughly disorientated and lost.

"This is so…" Tom did not know the words to explain how he felt. He was a simple man, living a simple and happy life. The only book Tom ever read was the Bible. His only education, fishing the oceans and growing vegetables. For him, that was the only essential knowledge he needed in life.

Alan didn't recognize me, he remembered.

He knew nothing of complicated scenarios, strange, unusual storms, or even how the fish in the sea might have died. He did not for one second understand what was happening to him. He lacked even the spark of an idea.

He opened the door to the cabin and saw his village.

Relief flooded him so much he sagged against the doorframe.

People were walking around, busy with their lives, and he knew each one of them very well. They'd all help him, he knew that. They were his friends.

There was little Mary, skipping along with a doll clutched tightly in her hand, and her mother, Anna, not far behind her.

"Anna!" He yelled and stumbled over.

Instead of seeing sympathy in her eyes, he saw fear. He stopped, confused all over again.

"There was a terrible storm," Tom said. "Where's Heather? Is she all right? She must be worried. Why isn't she here?"

"I'm sorry, I don't know you," Anna said and stepped back.

"Anna! No! You've known me your whole life!" Tom cried. "What is this madness?"

He stepped back, unable to process what was happening. Anna's expression of fright, the way she pushed her daughter behind her, and away from Tom.

What was going on? What did it all mean?

"I… I… Need…"

Tom stopped. He had no idea what to say.

He only knew he needed to see his wife. Quickly, he turned and ran. He weaved through the village, ignoring the shouts and gasps of surprise. He had to get to her, he had to get to his wife.

There. There was his small home, with smoke pouring from the chimney.

"Heather!" He yelled. "Heather, it's me!"

He raced up the twisted path, the one he laid with his very own hands. The door opened slowly, his heart began to soar. If he could just see her, just hold her, everything would be fine again.

A tall man stood in the doorway, the sheer size of him filled the narrow gap. Tom had never set eyes on the man before.

"Who the hell are you?" the man growled. "And why are you shouting for my wife?"

"I'm… She's… What?"

Is this some terrible joke? One the entire village must be in on? This is impossible.

"Please," Tom begged. "I don't understand. Where's Heather?"

The big man crossed his arms and snarled.

"I don't know you," a woman's soft voice spoke.

Heather, and truly, the woman was Heather, pushed around the big man and looked Tom straight in the eye. She stepped forward slowly. Tom gasped in horror. It was her, but she wasn't pregnant, wasn't the same at all. She wore her hair very differently, loose, and in waves. A style she'd always hated. His wife, but yet not his wife. She wore different clothes, even her posture was altered.

She doesn't know me. No, no, no!

His heart smashed into a thousand pieces. For the first time, he wondered if he'd died on the boat and was currently a resident of Hell.

"Hey!" a deep voice boomed behind him. "Who are ya? Why ya runnin' bout all over our village!"

Alan again.

Now Tom's sanity pinged apart and began to unwind. The impossible was occurring right before his eyes, and he had no way to explain any of it.

"Help me," Tom pleaded. "I woke up in your house and…"

"Whatcha doin' in my house!" Alan roared.

"You rescued me!"

"Dunno whatcha talkin' bout," he snapped back.

"The trawler. The storm, the fish!" Tom yelled.

"You're a madman!" Alan said.

Tom fell to his knees, openly sobbing in pain.

"Get outta here!" the big man in the doorway shouted. "Get away from us!"

"You're scaring me," Heather wailed and slammed the door.

Tom screamed. Screamed in bitter agony.

Fear, confusion, and terror battled for first place in his mind and body. No area of his own brain could comprehend his situation. Tom stood and did the only thing he could think to do. He ran.

***

Something happened in that storm. I could steal a boat and find it again? Or maybe I'm in the wrong village? No, that's impossible. A village full of identical people. It's madness. Maybe I'm mad. That has to be it.

Tom found the thought of insanity comforting. Surely that meant that there might be a cure? A way back to himself.

He sat alone on the shoreline, gazing out at the sea he once loved. He had no clear idea of what to do. In the naked light of day, he saw the village boats all collected and clustered together near the dock. His own boat, his father's, the one he'd been pulled in on, was gone. Vanished.

Why doesn't anyone know me? Alan did. Or at least, in this place, he met me at Father's trawler. So why did he forget me again? Heather was pregnant, eight months pregnant, and now she isn't. Oh God, help me. Please help me!

Wait, God, the church. Father Micheals might help.

Of course, he will. He always helps everyone.

Tom stood and brushed his clothes free of sand. The church, with its wooden safe walls and single bell, was in sight, tucked away at the back of the village.

He walked slowly, hunger and thirst twisted inside him. He avoided other villagers, kept his head down to avoid the narrow-eyed stares of everyone he'd known his entire life.

They all think I'm mad. Maybe I am! Tom fought off the wild urge to laugh.

He opened the church door quietly and stepped inside.

Father Micheals was there, Tom would recognize him anywhere. He busied himself cleaning the pulpit with an old rag. He turned and offered a smile and a graceful nod of his head.

"Father," Tom spoke. "Do you know me?"

Please say yes, please.

Father Micheals removed his glasses from a pocket and put them on, squinted, and frowned.

"I'm sorry, young man. If I do, I've quite forgotten!" He said and chuckled.

Tom's heart sank. The man of God was his last chance. It seemed pointless to explain now, pointless to even try.

Weariness overcame him. Utter defeat took hold.

"Can I sit for a while, please?"

He had nowhere else to go.

"Of course," Father Micheals answered. "Would you like a drink?"

The offer of such kindness brought fresh tears to Tom's eyes. He swallowed the lump in his throat and nodded.

I can't be in Hell. There wouldn't be any churches in Hell. The Bible says it's all fire and brimstone. Screams and sinners. So where am I? Where's my father? My Heather?

Tom rubbed his temples and sobbed loudly. It was all just too much, more than he could stand. He thought over his life. He'd never been a bad man. He'd never spoken badly to anyone or ever hurt a soul. Never even thought of doing such things. So why him? Why was he being forgotten, deleted? Or had he been replaced, or had the villagers been replaced?

Nothing made sense to him. None of it.

"Hello, who are you?" Father Micheals appeared and asked.

"You know me, I mean, no. Sorry, we just met. You said I could have a drink."

"Did I?"

"Yes, Father."

Father Micheals smiled and disappeared into another room. Tom could hear the clink of glasses, then stillness.

The sound of swirling material signaled his arrival again.

"Hello," he said. "Who are you?"

No one can remember me. No one. I'm being extinguished like a candle. Removed from memories.

"Father, please. We just met."

"Did we!"

"Yes. You went to... no, never mind."

Father Micheals returned to his scrubbing.

Tom sat and gazed around the church. It was a simple building, made of wood and painted white. A large crucifix, pulpit, and pews were the only real decorations.

Am I safe here? I must be. He sighed with temporary relief. He just needed to think, just needed space and time to think.

Father Micheals turned and stared at him.

"Hello," he said. "Who are you?"

Tom felt vomit rise. He pinched his skin firmly, reassured himself he was still real, still flesh and blood.

I need to find a boat. I need to find the storm. I need to go home. My real home and find my real wife. I can't let this beat me. Whatever this is.

He scrambled up, suddenly sure of his destination and plan. A small boat, that's all he needed. He'd never stolen before, but surely God would understand his urgency. He'd go back to where it all started. Before he became so lost and afraid. Before he became a stranger in his own village.

Tom opened the church doors and glimpsed the perfect sunshine.

Villagers passing saw the church doors open. A few stopped to stare. For a moment, it looked as if a small thin stranger, with wild hair, stood in the entrance. A trick of the light, they all presumed. That was all.

"Must be the wind!" Father Micheals laughed as he appeared and closed the doors. It had to be, after all, he was alone in the church. No one had been in for hours.

Tom Pritchard, a man lost somewhere in time and space. Stuck in a dimension that was not his own. Erased and scrubbed from existence.

A man on the verge of insanity, a stranger in a most familiar land. A man removed from reality, trapped in a realm he had never existed in.

Might a person slip through the cracks of reality? And might the universe find a way to correct its mistake, rectify its glitch... Somehow...

Tom Pritchard.
Occupation, Lost fisherman
Destination, deletion.

A TOURISTS GUIDE TO THE GALAXY

Meet Laklor. Age: Two hundred and seventeen. Origin: The peaceful planet of Zoriah, located in the constellation known as Aries.

Occupation: Tourist, travel advisory specialist, journalist. Collector of information.

A being on a lonely journey, traveling the galaxies, searching for the next great holiday spot.

Destination: Earth. Nevada.

Earth Year: 1979

Laklor didn't crash, like so many other races before it had. The landing was just a little bumpy, that was all.

A brief scan told it the vast desert might be the safest place to set its interstellar vehicle down, not that any humans might come looking. No, the moment the ship entered the atmosphere, it became invisible to human eyes. Shielded by technology and kept it off the limited human visual range.

Laklor wasn't stupid, absolutely not. Laklor had done its research on Earth.

The planet, located third rock from the sun, was being scouted for its potential as a holiday destination.

Laklor hoped to find compassionate human beings, with kindness as the main trait. It already knew what it should disguise itself as, in order to blend in. In its ship, it carried appropriate clothing for the many planets on its list and suitable money for each or trade items.

It chose a human male shape, age thirty as its mask.

Twenty-four earth hours were allowed before its report would be due.

Laklor left with a spring in its step, feeling hopeful and optimistic.

***

Laklor returned early, confused and deeply troubled.

Laklor filed its report.

Dearest readers,

Earth is the subject of today's article. Location, the third rock from the sun in the solar system we know as PrionX. A quick fly-by revealed a most beautiful planet. Almost a third is water. The rest consists of land, rather overtaken by jagged tall, sharp metallic buildings and each with human beings packed tightly together inside.

Each one has a small box to live in and use as a nest.

There appears to be a great disparity between Earth lands.

The human beings do not view themselves as one world, but rather as individual chunks of, what they call, nations. These nations are divided by invisible lines called 'Borders'.

Quite often, these nations go to war. Over what, it is hard to say or even comprehend. Some nations are wealthy in money (yes, there are some planets that still use this outdated method)

And some nations have almost nothing. Many starve whilst others live in luxury. Sharing must be against human nature I feel.

There exists a multitude of religions, worshipping various deities. Rather than become a species that might embrace and learn each other's belief system, humans argue over whose invisible God is real and whose invisible God might be better or might possess more invisible powers. This has caused countless historical, and no doubt, future wars.

The oceans are being poisoned, the vast and varied marine life and animal life are heading towards complete extinction. Pollution is rife, as is disease.

Human beings swarm and reproduce rapidly. In a bacterial-like fashion.

I disembarked my vehicle, still feeling optimistic.

I chose a male human as my disguise and left my ship to head to what is called a 'TRUCK STOP DINER.'

The sand of the desert felt glorious in my new borrowed hands. Warm and soft, a simple overlooked pleasure.

The humans have strips of what they term 'Roads,' with primitive machinery driven on top, machinery they sit inside to travel. They still use fossil fuels (Humans are not an advanced race)

The desert has been sliced open by these crude roads.

The roads themselves are difficult to cross. Signs show that there is at least a speed limit. But humans don't pay attention to those signs, so they are, in fact, quite pointless.

On entering the establishment, I was greeted with cool air and a piece of slippery paper handed to me by a female in a uniform. On it listed the food they had for sale (There is no trading system) This was called a 'Menu.'

There is no guide as to what ingredients the food might consist of. I was led to what is termed a 'Booth.' The female poured me what she called a 'Coffee.'

This appears to be a standard beverage.

I observed other patrons with their own coffee drinks. Some added small white crystals, a sweet substance, and some added the juice of a cow. A cow is an Earth animal and one most humans also eat.

I added both the cow juice and crystals. Now, this is where I made a crucial first mistake. The female observed me drinking the beverage in one gulp, which was very hot, almost boiling, in fact. This was not appropriate for Earth, as she showed great shock. One should sip the drink in order to blend in.

Anything out of the ordinary appears to frighten human beings greatly. They are easily spooked.

Next came a pie, made of Earth apples, a fruit. I was given a curious implement in order to eat this, a clumsy metallic object with prongs.

This proved most difficult. One must stab the food, piece by piece, and insert the food into one's mouth, chew and swallow.

A piece of rough paper is given, should you wish to remove it from said mouth. Which I did.

"Is everything okay?" The female asked.

She showed concern towards me and this action gave me brief hope. I nodded and asked to pay. More difficulty ensued. Earth money features portraits of special men long ago dead. Their Gods perhaps? A curious way to honor.

One can have metal coins or thin paper notes. The more an Earth person has of the coins and notes, the more respected and liked they are.

After some difficulty, the female helped me arrange my money into an order. I paid, anxious to leave.

Through the doors came a man wearing a star-shaped badge. These are the leaders of Earth. If a person is seen doing something against their set laws, they are snatched by this group and put in a metal barred box called a 'Cell.'

In the small car park were many metal vehicles. I approached each one and inquired over where might be best to visit. Two humans were extremely rude and used particular words to show they were not impressed with my questions. The words were Fuck and Off. The guttural word 'Fuck,' was not in my database.

Humans, it seems, are rather odd.

One female told me a place called 'Las Vegas' might be to my liking. She told me I needed to catch what they called a 'Bus.'

This is a most peculiar invention. After some observation, I learned one should not reach out and physically 'catch' the bus, but rather a person must stand close to a certain sign and climb into a large machine on wheels, usually packed full of other people. You must give money to the person behind another wheel and sit down very still. The journey then commences.

As we sped along, I sat and listened to many conversations around me.

It seems humans are fond of holidays too. Not for purposes of exploration, but for fun.

A drink often made of fermented yeast, essentially a poison, is consumed. This alters human behavior if taken in large quantities. A person then acts very differently, inhibitions are lost. The poison leads a person to do wild things, wake up very sick due to dehydration, and with no memory of the night before. A person then repeats the process.

This is earth fun for the majority.

A most strange occurrence and one I still don't quite have an answer for.

Las Vegas came into sight. Built in the middle of the desert, it features tall inelegant buildings decorated with lights. A shimmery blight on an otherwise beautiful landscape.

Many humans choose to visit.

As we dismounted the bus, people were eager to get inside the buildings. They pushed and shoved until they were first. Perhaps it was a race?

I remain unsure.

First, I saw a group of males. Loud and excited. I watched, curious, and followed.

They each drank the poisoned beverage and encouraged each other to do so quickly. Another race?

I soon learned they were on what is called a "bachelor weekend."

This occurs before the union of two humans, most often a male and female. A man takes a weekend to behave quite curiously before he is tied down by the female.

I presume this means to be willingly captured and tied to a surface to ensure he cannot escape. Females also do this rather bizarre ritual too. One group decorated themselves with pictures of a male's sexual anatomy. They also tend to scream loudly.

These groups frequent 'Clubs,' where more drinks are consumed and a mating ritual dance is performed. This involves human beings moving in odd ways to loud thumping music, in order to lure their chosen mate.

All very crude and, frankly, disturbing.

Mating rituals on earth require further study.

Inside the main 'Casino' buildings, people give their money away, money they have saved or perhaps stolen, hoping to be given more in return. They take what is called a 'Risk' Or, a 'Gamble.'

Often, they leave with nothing at all. They can be found outside, wandering the busy streets in a state of despair and leaking clear fluid from their eyes.

People feed large machinery with metal coins, hoping the machines might feel overfed and vomit.

For a time, I wandered, trying to make sense of the sights before me. The buildings were loud and full of smoke. Arguments often broke out over small, very minor things. I assume it was the effects of the poison drinks.

There were also drugs consumed. More toxic substances, chemical in nature and used to alter behavior.

Females with painted faces and limbs on display walked around and offered drinks or plastic discs called chips. Here I made a second mistake. I knew the word chip, so I assumed the discs were food. They were not.

You must give money, in order to buy chips. You then gamble them away and are left with nothing.

I observed one female win more chips than anyone else. She then proceeded to give them all back.

I left. Confused. Wondering what the purpose of it all appeared to be.

Outside, night had fallen.

The stars were on display and yet, no one stopped to look above. I wandered a place named 'The Strip' and observed behavior.

Humans, it seemed to me, were rude, obnoxious, and rather callous.

If a person happened to stumble, people watched them fall, rather than help. They then laughed at another's misfortune.

There is a delightful complement of skin colors in humans, all wonderful, quite remarkable shades. Those with darker skin colors seem to be treated as less. Which was rather baffling nonsense.

The female of the species is also treated as lesser, which is again, most strange.

I found no real reason why this should be the case, only that it is.

Differences are sadly not embraced and treasured. No, it was quite the opposite.

As the night wore on, more humans behaved differently, through the effects of the poison drink, no doubt.

Fights broke out. The leaders in uniforms arrived to take the culprits and place them inside a box. Humans have to do what these leaders say, or they can be killed or hurt.

I wandered more. Some groups of people promoted 'Peace.'

The males wore their hair long and their intention was rather admirable. Other people, however, did not appreciate the groups.

Televisions. Some people sit and watch others in a play of some kind, and find entertainment in that. The plays are recorded in a studio and streamed over primitive airwaves.

The news is also popular.

Still, humans watch terrible things happen in other nations and shrug. They do nothing to help their own species.

Not many earth miles away from Las Vegas sits a secret base of test aircraft. The people of the nation pay towards the upkeep of the base via a tax system, but they are not allowed to know where their money is going. It is confidential.

I presume the secret aircraft are to fight in wars.

This is a planet that has only recently discovered atomic energy. As soon as the power was developed, they harnessed the energy into a highly destructive bomb and destroyed many people. The people who decided to drop the bomb were not put in a cell but thanked.

I appreciate this makes no sense at all.

Sounds, lights, noise. Unbearable bustle.

Sadly, I could not bear to stay.

I waited for a bus, only to be told there weren't any. Feeling desperate to escape the sin and corruption, I began to walk.

I decided that as soon as I was out of sight, I would discard my human disguise and race to my ship. I wanted nothing more than to leave the filthy planet and never return.

On the long road out, large machinery stopped.

"Do you want a ride?" A male human said.

I stopped, unsure of what a ride might entail. "Get in," he said, and so I did.

The following is a transcribe of the conversation we had as he drove.

The male: So, did you lose big? I recognize the look.

Me: Who's big?

The male: Ha hahaha. Fair enough. Where ya' heading?

Me: The desert, please.

The male: Where are you from? You sound funny.

Me: Someplace far away.

The male: Like Europe?

Me: Yes.

The Male: Well, I'm Jim.

Me: Hello Jim, I'm Laklor.

Jim: Not Russian, are you? Like a spy or something? They say we still need to worry about Russians.

Me: I'm just a tourist.

Jim: Haha. Did you like Vegas?

Me: No.

Jim: Yeah, me neither. Brings out the worst in folks.

Me: What are folks?

Jim: People. That's what I mean. Forget you're foreign, sorry.

Me: What is the best of folks? Where should I go to see that?

Jim: Well ain't you a strange one. Cities are all right sometimes. Vegas is just about the worst one to pick. Me, I'm passing through. I like to drive my truck at night while it's peaceful. All them stars to look at. Makes you wonder.

Me: Yes.

Jim: They reckon we'll get to Mars one day. What do you think about that?

Me: Humans should not be allowed to spread.

Jim: Christ! What a thing to say!

Me: There is a sickness of misery inside humans.

My temporary companion fell silent for two Earth minutes.

Jim: We ain't all bad. We got plenty of good in us. Folks like my wife, she looks after sick kids. Kids with diseases and me, I ain't never bin nothin' but fair!

Me: Diseases are obsolete where I come from. The notes you have, with the faces of your gods, you should use those to discover cures, instead of building special aircraft for wars.

Jim: No diseases? You sure you come from Europe?

Me: Yes.

Break for silence again. I could tell I had made my companion uncomfortable. Mistake number three.

Me: You can stop here, Jim.

Jim: We're in the middle of nowhere. It's not safe!

Me: I'll be fine. Thank you.

(I gave Jim my paper notes and metallic coins)

Jim: Woah! There are hundreds here. Are you sure about this? I was just giving you a lift for free. Wanted nothin' to happen to ya out walkin' by yourself.

Me: You were concerned? Kindness?

Jim: Yeah. Rest of America ain't like Vegas, you know. We're good folk.

Me: Thank you for the knowledge. Goodbye.

Jim: Wait, wait! You're in the desert. There's snakes and bad stuff.

Me: Yes. I've seen the bad. Goodbye Mr. Jim.

I walked away from the strange male with hair covering his face. After a few steps, he started up his machinery and left.

I had not used up my twenty-four earth hours. I discarded my disguise, glad to be free of the illusion, and arrived at my ship.

I sat quietly in contemplation before I decided to circle Earth.

I saw a great many things. More jagged cities. Ancient, dusty lands still standing, built by people long forgotten.

Rainforests are in the process of being destroyed by greed.

I witnessed several small groups living quite naturally alongside nature. Seemingly free, for the time being, of the plague that is humankind.

I saw animals of all types, too. Some were kept in boxes purely so human beings could visit and stare at them, or perhaps they had committed a crime and the boxes were their cells?

I found myself able to come to one conclusion only.

Reader.

Earth is to be avoided at all costs. It is no destination for exploration or curiosity. It is a place where to be different is to be in danger, where kindness is rare and strangers are feared.

A hollowness, a deep hole, lives in humankind. They fill that hole with terrible things.

The planet has topped the list of the ten most dangerous destinations.

Yours. Laklor

***

For the attention of High Command.

On the subject of Earth.

Out in the vast universe, as you all know, we have a rule on non-interference.

This is set for two reasons.

One, it is not our place to assist a world and its civilizations in its growing pains. We know this.

Two, a civilization such as Earth greatly fears anything different to themselves.

A ship entering their atmosphere, if seen, would be attacked without thought. This has unfortunately happened before. The remains of that ship lay in pieces in secret facilities, kept away from human eyes in case such sights might awaken wonders.

This is a mindset of the leaders, not necessarily of the people.

The people, it seems, are kept in a state of existence that suits only those leaders.

Fear of others, greed, poison drinking, taxes, earning, spending, gambling are encouraged. A society of materialism and greed.

A society whose deepest care is over what a person looks like and how much money they have. The majority care nothing for self-improvement.

Some, I admit, are quite different and are more advanced. For that reason, annihilation is not recommended. Yet.

However, there exists a sickness in humanity so great that their spread to other planets must be prevented. I assume they would attack and try to colonize other worlds.

I discovered, on my journey, that this will soon be the case. The planet Mars is their destination. If that occurs, what might stop them from spreading further?

It is highly recommended that Earth be very closely monitored. Steps should be taken to ensure they do not leave their own solar system unless a change of behavior occurs.

The majority are most hostile and graced with low intelligence while simultaneously believing themselves to be superior. A most dangerous mixture.

The majority also lack respect for anything less than material things.

I expect the many separate nations of Earth will only decline, although as always, I remain hopeful.

Yours. With deep regret.

Laklor.

Laklor left the solar system at an incomprehensible speed. For it, it couldn't leave fast enough. Laklor hoped it would never have to return.

Laklor. A lone traveler. An unhappy tourist.

A being with a single-minded focus, a deep determination to discover the very best holiday destinations.

Off the list. Planet Earth.
Classification. Avoid at all costs.
Possible future. Annihilation.

WRITTEN ON A SUBWAY WALL

Imagine, if you will, a prophecy. Not one found in dusty, ancient texts, but one from the mouth of a lone, frightened woman.

Premonitions, psychic powers, the ability to see what has not come to pass.

A future set in stone? A glimpse of likely events?

How can minds see what has not yet occurred for eyes?

What might one witness, when the fourth dimension shatters, its limits lifted and unrestricted? Limits removed by an extraordinary stranger.

Meet Ms. Carmen Russel, age thirty-five. A lonely woman, a calm, and loving soul. Hopelessly lost and afraid. Discarded by the society she adores.

A woman who longs for nothing more than four walls, one roof, and one warm bed. A chance to sleep in safety and comfort.

Carmen Russel, possible dreamer of future events?

Might knowledge of the future be found scribbled in a theoretical physicist's notes, or might it be scrawled on a subway wall for all to see?

A warning, gifted to one for the benefit of all…

Carmen pulled her thin blanket more tightly around herself and shivered. There was no more room in the overnight shelter. No place for her in its drafty halls and rooms. Soon, winter would arrive, and then what would she do?

Always alone, so desperately alone and entirely overlooked.

There were many nights in Carmen's life when her situation seemed beyond hopeless. Danger, threats, and chaos were never far. Safety, for her, was almost obsolete.

A full belly was a rarity, as was a roof over her head.

Trapped in a desperate spiral that seemed endless, she couldn't find a job without an address, and couldn't get an address without a job. Her own private circle of hell.

At age thirty-three, she had fled a vicious husband, fled a terrible marriage that had once provided love and sanctuary, only to end up homeless and alone. Trapped once more, a different kind of vicious cycle, her second private hell.

Carmen tried to look on the bright side of life, although her determination that one day she would be finally safe was fading rapidly.

The recent promise of help from a charity had fallen through and summer work that paid cash in hand was lesser every year. Carmen wasn't afraid of hard work, she thrived on working and helping others.

"It's too hopeless," she muttered.

Darkness was drawing close, which meant more danger without the protection of walls around her. Too exposed, too vulnerable, too afraid.

Some nights, she wandered on her lonesome, along quiet roads and empty streets. Never feeling safe enough to stop, always fearing the sound of quick footsteps close behind.

She huddled in a shop doorway and tried to keep away from the harsh wind. People rushed by, leaving workplaces. Hardly any ever looked her way. None ever dared to meet her eyes. They could all live with themselves if they refused to acknowledge her. They could all sleep at night in their comfortable beds, and eat their luxury food without guilt if people like Carmen were at the back of their minds.

On occasion, a kind stranger would pass her and offer a rare smile and a coin or two. Carmen was always extremely grateful to be seen.

Her plight was not unusual. Many homeless people clustered close by, but as a woman, life was automatically harsher, danger closer and more severe.

She closed her eyes briefly and wondered if she could sleep before the streets fell quiet. All day she had looked for work and had applied for housing and help yet again. No luck. Nothing.

Her stomach rumbled loudly. She curled herself into a ball and rested her head on a doorframe.

She felt exhausted. Weary and cold. Lonely too, forever lonely.

She had once been a girl with dreams and ambitions, hopes and goals. She yearned to be part of the vibrancy of life. Sadly, she remained unseen, unwanted.

Still, even though she felt the girl inside her was dead, killed by the harshness of life. The woman, the woman inside her, fought tooth and claw.

One day, she thought. One day I'll be safe and warm in a bed of my own.

A brief flash of white disturbed her thoughts.

Lightning? A camera flash? No, only an endless stream of people rushing by. None had noticed the odd burst of brightness.

Wait.

Who was that standing on the opposite side of the street? An absurdly tall man wearing a fitted suit stood watching her.

Carmen squinted and assumed his impossible height was a trick of the light. An illusion and no more. It looked as if his arms were so long that they trailed down to his thighs.

No one is that tall! He's almost as big as the streetlight.

She rubbed her eyes and looked once more. No one stood staring. The man was gone.

She shook her head and tried desperately to find comfort on the hard, damp steps.

A curious, warm feeling began to engulf her. She nestled down in her blanket, tired all the way into her bones.

In her mind, she imagined sleeping in a warm bed. Safe and unbothered, alone to dream in comfort. She had forgotten how such a thing could feel. She recalled from her childhood, warm meadows drenched in sunlight, the sweet smell of freshly mowed grass, the feel of warm sand on her bare feet...

Carmen slept. Carmen dreamed.

***

Big Ben chimed twelve and the Autumn day was crisp and bright. In her dream, Carmen walked a path close to the Thames. She wore the same clothing in her dreams as in life and carried the same worn-out bag. Leaves crunched loudly under her mismatched boots.

In her hands she gripped an old newspaper filled with chips—the scent of salt and vinegar made her mouth water. She used a wooden chip fork to eat, the food warm in her belly. A man jogged past listening to thudding music. He wore huge headphones and almost crashed into her.

"Hey! Look where you're going!" He shouted, even though he was the one at fault.

Carmen shook her head and sat on a bench alone to eat, pleased she'd had enough coins to buy warm food.

The strange roaring sound started minutes after. First, she glanced around and noticed people looking up, some pointed at the sky in shock and despair.

Carmen followed their gazes and saw a huge airplane descending rapidly. Thick black smoke billowed from one of its engines.

She knew it was about to crash, destined to plummet down. The plane was dropping at high speed, nose-first. The sound was horrendous and gut-wrenching. People were screaming and wailing in terror. A few stood and recorded the events with their cell phones. Carmen jumped to her feet, knocking her precious chips all over the ground.

Somewhere in the distance, sirens began to blare.

The plane stuttered, plunged, and crashed in a fury of noise. A huge fireball exploded almost immediately, directly in the center of London's busiest streets. The scene melted away and was replaced.

She dreamed she was running towards London Bridge, racing to help, screaming 'No, no. no,' in disbelief as she fled. Frantic in her need to help others. Fuelled by an urgency.

In the next scene, she held a metal pipe in her hand and understood she had found it for a reason. Knew she needed it.

Heart-wrenching screams penetrated her mind. Fire and smoke billowed.

***

Carmen jolted awake. She was sweating in the cold. Disorientated, she blinked quickly and jerked. For a moment, her mind was filled with the need to save people hurt in the terrible accident.

It's not real, it's just a dream. Just a dream, she told herself.

But of course, things are rarely ever that simple.

For the entire morning, her head ached. A remnant from the strange dream or maybe from the angle of her neck as she slept, she wasn't sure.

She couldn't shake the traumatic scenes. Every time she closed her eyes she could picture the plane as it struggled, saw the flames as it dived down out of control.

She decided to walk, to find someplace else to sit. Maybe she could watch the world go by without her, maybe she could find a bed for the night in one of the shelters.

As she strolled, she headed towards the Thames, a path she'd walked many times and the same one she had chosen in her dream.

A small white van sold fish and chips from a counter, wrapped in what looked like old newspaper. Carmen thought it was a charming sight and smiled.

Her stomach picked that moment to remind her she desperately needed food. She checked her donated coins. Yes, she had enough for a small bag. Thrilled, she joined the short queue eagerly.

People turned to stare at her, as they so often did. Always the same expression on their faces, one of disgust, as if her lifestyle were from her own making, her own design.

Head down, feeling shame, she waited, paid, and walked away.

The feeling of déjà vu hit her strongly, so much so that it almost knocked her off balance. For a second, she smiled, lost in the coincidence and nothing more.

I must be more tired than I thought.

Still, she felt happy with her temporary pleasure of chips. She poked the hot food with her wooden fork and walked as she ate.

A man jogged past wearing large headphones and almost crashed into her.

"Hey! Look where you're going!" He called.

Carmen stopped. The feeling of nausea and shock began to swirl. A strange, almost out-of-body feeling.

No, it's impossible. It can't be.

The entire scene, she had lived it before, hadn't she?

The very same events played out in real life as the ones in her dreams had.

Quickly, she spotted a bench and sat. Her hands were shaking violently. She placed her chips in their newspaper on her knee and rubbed her temples.

It's just a coincidence. Visions aren't real. It was just a dream.

When she heard the cries of distress and the sound of a struggling engine roaring above her head, she found she didn't need to look up. No, she knew what happened next.

Chaos. Brutal unimaginable chaos.

Screaming and wailing, pounding footsteps, and crying sounds. She braced herself for the explosion she knew with fierce certainty she would hear.

BOOM.

The plane hit the exact place she dreamt of. The busy center of London. The huge fireball stormed the sky. Thick black smoke appeared. She stood and dropped her food. Pulled her hair and yanked, unsure of what to do.

"No, no!" she cried. Her mind filled with pain and shock. Despair and confusion.

Around her, people ran. Carmen joined the surge before she realized what she was doing.

She had to help. She had to help people. She must.

Others had the very same thoughts. She followed the crowds, this time equal to one of them.

The scene across the bridge looked like an apocalypse had occurred. Thick acrid smoke filled the air. Somewhere, an engine still powered loudly. Buildings were reduced to rubble, cars were flattened. People were screaming and small fires were bursting out everywhere. Fire engines, police, and paramedics rushed by. It seemed an impossibility to get close enough to help victims of the plane crash.

"This way," a man yelled to others. "Help me with them."

Powered by adrenaline, Carmen didn't hesitate.

People were trapped in an upstairs block in a building on fire. Frantic faces clustered around a smashed window. A car, likely thrown by the force of the crash, blocked the doorway like a discarded toy.

The man ran down a small alleyway and yanked on a chained-closed fire door. Thudding came from behind. He started kicking relentlessly. Carmen joined him.

The door wouldn't break, only cracked.

She knew better than anyone, the things that might lay abandoned in derelict alleyways. Besides, hadn't she seen what to do already?

The realization hit.

She fled, searching the ground as she ran. A wooden plank, no. A spanner, no. There, an old heavy metal pipe, the one from her dream. She grabbed it and raced back.

"Use this," she gasped. "The chain."

The man did as he was told. With the force of both of them, the chain broke apart after a short battle.

Smoke poured out. The man ran inside and up a short staircase. Carmen followed, her old scarf around her mouth.

Within seconds, her eyes stung and she found herself choking.

People, a whole group, saw their approach and sank with relief. Carmen gripped an injured woman and half dragged her outside, back into the chaotic street.

"OUT," a police officer called and pointed. "Everyone that way now! Get out!"

"There are people," Carman gasped. "Stuck,"

The woman in her arms was bleeding furiously. Pools of blood covered her clothing.

"Help me," she whimpered.

Carmen dragged her to the end of the road, her chest heaving. Hundreds of people stood behind a clumsily erected barricade. Arms reached for the woman, arms reached for her.

Carmen fell onto the pavement, coughing heavily. Loud voices and shouts pierced her mind. Her vision swam. Someone patted her back, tried to lift her to her feet. A glimpse at the crowd revealed him.

The tall man, the impossibly tall man in the suit, watched her struggle.

She tried to shout, tried to speak. Dizziness overcame her, her heartbeat thudded relentlessly in her ears.

The last things she saw were shoes and boots. She realized she was on the ground and then only blackness surrounded her.

***

Carmen lay on a trolley in a busy hospital corridor. Shock and smoke inhalation, they said. She kept her eyes closed and listened to the chorus of sounds around her. It was the frantic cries of horror and pain that rose above the rest of the noise.

Could I have stopped it? Was there time? There must be so many injured.

She felt the trolley she lay on being moved and tried to remove her oxygen mask, intent on telling someone, anyone, what she had seen.

"Please," she said. Her voice was hoarse and ruined. An orderly bent down to listen.

"Please, I saw it happen," she said.

"Lots of people did sweetheart, it was a terrible crash."

"No, please, before, I saw it before."

"I'm taking you to a ward."

The orderly placed the mask back over Carmen's face. Exhaustion gripped her. Her chest hurt, her body ached. Her mind felt as if it were on fire with flames of disbelief. The movements of the trolley lulled her, soothed her.

Everything was okay, she was being taken care of. She would explain later. Someone would listen, they had to. Someone would know what to do.

Her sore eyes closed as the trolley stopped. Another blanket was placed over her body. Warmth. Safety. The two things she so desperately craved.

Dreams soon followed.

***

Carmen dreamed of walking along the deck of a huge ship. The air felt tangy with salt and sunshine. People lay on sunloungers, relaxed and happy, sipping drinks in tall glasses. Others walked by hand in hand, all smiles.

Feeling excited, she ran to the side rails and peered over. She was on a ship of some magnitude. An ocean liner, a cruise ship. Carmen had never been on a ship. She watched the choppy waters and stillness of the ocean in the distance.

How did I get here?

It was then she realized she was in a dream. An invisible passenger, yet the ship felt vivid and alive for her. She heard multiple conversations and talks of a tour at the next stop, Greece.

She touched her fingers, pinched herself. The sharp feeling of pain made her gasp.

I can feel! Can I explore?

She spun around, eager to sightsee, and raced across the deck. Her hospital gown flapped in the wind.

Why am I wearing this?

She shrugged and gazed around.

Elegant stenciled writing announced the ship was called 'The Genevieve.'

What a pretty name. I wonder if I can...

A massive explosion sounded. The jolt caused Carmen to fall onto her hands and knees. The entire ship lurched in protest and tipped to one side. The awful deafening sound of grinding metal. Commotion and chaos.

Screams of terror and confusion that were now so familiar rang out. Sickness rose inside of her.

Was the ship going to sink? What would happen to her and everyone onboard?

People pounded past her, frantic and frightened. Somewhere, a child screamed for its mother. Carmen tried to climb to her feet and felt another heavy lurch as the ship tipped.

It's sinking.

She crawled up the deck, latching on through sheer force until she could haul herself up on the railings. From her position, the view of the ocean was gone, replaced with the clear blue sky. An impossibly beautiful day for a disaster.

Her arms ached from the force of her grip. Water splashed in her face, again the taste of salt. A piercing loud metallic grinding sounded.

Carmen screamed.

***

"Hush, it's just a dream."

A nurse stood by her side in a dark ward. Not on a ship, still in the hospital. Not dying and drowning, but in a bed, safe.

"I... There was a... ship!"

"Just a dream, go back to sleep. You were screaming."

Shaken, Carmen squeezed her eyes shut and rolled onto her side.

No one will believe me. Of course not. Think, what can I do?

She knew it was the middle of the night. For once, she was safe in a bed, walls around her.

Maybe this is a breakdown? That's what this is.

She felt around inside herself for the truth, her instinct. She saw the plane crash before it occurred and assumed it was a dream until it happened. Now a ship. What was its name? Did she see? She wracked her mind for an answer. Recalled the images. Yes, the ship was called The Genevieve. Carmen knew one other thing. She was glimpsing the future and she knew she must be seeing it for a reason.

In the morning, a kind nurse found some clean clothes for her. Simple, tired-out jogging bottoms, a t-shirt, and shoes that barely fit.

Carmen felt better physically. Her mind, however, was in turmoil.

"I can't let you go until a doctor has seen you," the nurse said.

Carmen nodded and smiled.

"Can I just go outside for some air? Ten minutes, that's all," she lied.

"Sure you can. I'll find you a jumper. It's cold today."

Carmen had a plan and she needed to leave. First, she planned on finding the newspaper offices, failing that, the police. Or should it be the other way around?

She made her way to the lift area, a large borrowed jumper clutched in her hand. She shrugged it over her head and stepped inside the lift. The doors opened and stopped to let others inside. Everyone talked constantly of the plane crash.

"Engine failure," someone said. "Or a bomb, I bet."

"They say hundreds died, maybe a thousand."

On the ground floor, the hospital was jammed. Outside stood reporters.

Carmen's mind sparked with a new idea.

A white van with a satellite on top was parked in the waiting area. Carmen crossed over and tapped a cameraman on the back.

"Excuse me, I saw the crash," she said. "I helped at the scene."

"Did you! Hang on. Kate, you might want to talk to this lady."

A smartly dressed woman appeared. She held out a perfectly manicured hand and smiled.

"Can I interview you?" She asked. "You were on the scene, right?"

"Yes, please," Carmen answered.

"What's your name?"

"Carmen."

Don't do this, they'll never believe you. Walk away.

Before she had time to think, a camera was focused on her face. The smart woman, Kate, smoothed her jacket down and introduced her.

"So, Carmen. The plane accident has made global news and you were on the scene, is that correct?"

"Yes, I helped trapped people in a building, and I…"

"That's very brave of you. Londoners rushing to help each other. What was it like and how many were injured?"

Carmen gulped. Her mouth felt dry, nerves wracked her stomach. She shivered even though sweat poured down her spine and made her flinch.

I shouldn't do this. They'll lock me up.

The thought of being locked away suddenly soothed her. She wouldn't have to deal with anyone then, wouldn't have to worry about where she was going to sleep or what she was going to eat. Her safety would be guaranteed, surely. But, no, she had to try. People depended on her even if they didn't know it. The ship in her dreams was full. Packed full of innocent families.

Just try. Try hard.

"It was awful, smoke and fire and screaming. I helped a woman and then… but you see, I saw it happen. Before it happened, I mean."

"I'm sorry what?" Kate frowned.

"I dreamed about it. The night before it happened. A cruise ship explodes soon, The Genevieve, on its way to Greece and it sinks really fast, so I think…"

"Cut!"

Shit, what did I expect? They think I'm mad.

"Whatever ward you've come from, I suggest you go back and get help," Kate snapped. "We've no time for shit like this."

Carmen opened her mouth and closed it. She knew the looks they were giving her, that distasteful look as if they'd each swallowed something unpleasant. She was used to stares like that.

Slowly, she backed up and walked away.

The tall suited man stood half-hidden behind a car, gazing and staring at her. She couldn't see his face, only two dark pits for eyes. Long arms dragged by his sides.

Carmen shuddered and ran.

***

No one at the two main newspaper offices wanted to help. Both receptionists threatened to call mental health services. The police station was full of people. All the same, Carmen joined the queue, only to be told to stop wasting time or risk arrest.

She made her way across London, stopping to stare at newspaper headlines announcing the terrible plane crash to the world.

She had been lost inside for the majority of her life, yet she had never felt so out of place.

Where can I go? Who can I tell? Travel agents? No. What can I do?

Carmen longed to be around people. Around the vibrancy and chaos people brought. She feared the tall man. The tall, silent man in his impeccable suit.

She headed to the busy subway system.

She couldn't get through the gates without a pass, so she sat on a bench and watched the life around her.

Londoners carried on as normal, despite the catastrophe.

She cared about all of them. Every resilient stranger. Even though none gave her a second look, and if they did, it was one of disgust. She held her head in her hands and sobbed. The things she'd seen, the horrors and desperation. And one event hadn't even happened yet.

What could she do? Social media might be worth a try, but she had no accounts and no phone.

Someone at the homeless shelter? Would they help? As people rushed by, she realized she was one of the unseen lost. Avoided and given a wide berth.

That might give her an advantage for her sudden idea. A small shop caught her eye. She went in and did something she had never done before. She stole.

Although her own hunger raged, she picked up a single black marker pen and left.

On a blank tiled wall in the subway station, she wrote.

'Ocean liner The Genevieve will suffer from a huge explosion and sink near Greece soon. Spread the word. Stop it before it happens. Please.'

Although a few sets of curious eyes watched her. None interfered. She left as she arrived, unnoticed.

That night, the cold was worse. Damp seeped its way into her bones. The jumper didn't do much to help. She shivered grimly and failed to wipe away the tears that ran down her face.

Why do I try to help others when no one helps me? Who can I go to?

Carmen felt exhausted but afraid to sleep. The hour was late and the streets were quiet. Only the sound of people leaving busy pubs broke the silence. Carmen had written her prophecy on several subway walls, on bus stop shelters, on low billboards, on every place she could reach until the pen ran dry.

In her mind, if she could stop just one person from getting on that ship, then the dreams were for a reason.

It seemed to her that the visions that lay cluttered in her mind were more about inflicting cruelty on her.

She wiped her face, tucked her hair behind her ears, and decided to walk.

Wait.

He was there. Standing on the opposite side of the street was the solitary tall man. His long arms hung all the way down to his knees, his fingers twitched. He watched her watch him.

"What do you want me to do?!" Carmen raged. "No one believes me!"

He shook his head slowly from side to side. Not mocking, but sad.

Disappointment in herself took hold.

"What can I do?" She cried. "I'm no one! You did this! Who are you?! Why me?"

The man slowly melted away. He did not step back or forward, he simply extinguished like a light.

"I don't know what to do!" Carmen shouted after him. "Nobody hears me!"

An idea flickered. She grabbed it with both hands and followed the train of thought.

Head down, she walked until she found a working phone box. She dialed the emergency services.

"I know someone who put a bomb on the British cruise ship, The Genevieve. It's going to explode close to Greece."

She laid the phone back down gently.

Would it be enough to stop the accident? Would the huge search they'd have to do show damage somewhere?

She walked away. Deep down she felt the call wasn't enough, knew it wasn't.

All night Carmen wandered. She wished she would have taken the time to enjoy the hospital bed more. Or stayed until the food was served, at least.

Had she been given a blessing or a curse?

Wasn't she cursed enough already?

She wandered lonely streets and quiet suburbs until her feet ached. She found herself on a high street. Cafes were opening, another day was starting. She could smell food and fresh bread cooking. The cozy scent made her stop and cry.

A young woman watched her for a moment as she arranged a sign in the dark street. She disappeared and returned with a hot drink and a paper bag full of food.

"Here, have this," she told her.

The act of kindness made Carmen sob harder.

"Is there anything I can do, sweetheart?" The woman asked.

"No. I don't think so. Thank you so much."

People like the woman were the reason Carmen still had the greatest of faith in humanity.

She took her treats to a small park, drank, and ate until the sun came up.

From behind a tree, the tall, suited man watched her. This time, Carmen ignored him.

She felt too afraid to sleep. Too frightened to dream. Her body disagreed. Weariness overcame her. She curled herself into a ball, surrounded by people in a busy park, and slept.

***

In her dream, she wandered a dark city, one full of neon signs and life. A full moon hung in the sky.

Where am I now?

There were plenty of bars, packed with people enjoying drinks with friends, overflowing restaurants too. Fancy cars rushed past, all shiny and new. Carmen could sense the wealth. A great big divide between her and them.

She walked further, almost gliding on an invisible set path. Past expensive jewelry stores, past car showrooms, onto more bars and restaurants.

L.A.'s finest steaks, a sign told her.

As soon as the knowledge landed, the ground began to shake. The sidewalks undulated and spasmed.

Alarms sounded, then came the screaming. People flooded out of buildings as the path began to shake faster, harder. The sensation reminded her of a ride she once went on at a funfair in her childhood.

Earthquake.

A woman close by fell to her knees, whole groups staggered and crashed down like bowling pins, shook by the fierce motion. Cars collided, thrown into one another's paths. A building cracked. The ground would not cease its movements, only became more frantic.

The sidewalk cracked apart, entire stores broke in two as if chopped down the middle.

Slabs of concrete fell from the sky, falling straight off buildings, debris swirled. Dust and terror.

Panic rose inside herself. She screamed a wail of fright until she awoke.

***

Carmen sat panting on the bench. Gasping for breath. People walked past and stared at her.

Every time I sleep. I can't take this anymore. I can't.

She stood on limbs that were too shaky to hold her. In the corner of her eye, the tall, suited man stood, half-hidden behind a tree. Emotionless, ever watchful, never blinking.

"Stop!" Carmen shouted. "Stop doing this to me!"

She had to get away. Had to get away from him.

She ran, her feet pounded the pavement. She had no idea of where to run to, where to go. She only knew she needed to get away and do so quickly.

Sounds around her became her enemy. It was all too much, too loud. The fear she felt in her dream had stayed with her. Disorientated, she raced across the park, heading for the busy streets full of traffic.

There had to be someone, someone who could help, someone who could make it stop. She just had to find them.

The screech of brakes sounded. Carmen felt the impact of a car. With a sense of almost calm detachment, she understood she'd been hit.

Agony burst across her leg, her head pierced with pain.

Faces peered at her, images blurred.

Am I dying? Is this it?

Shouts for help rang out. Was it her shouting, or someone else? She found she couldn't tell.

Reality became twisted. Dreams into life and life into dreams.

"Earthquake," she mumbled. "Earthquake soon." She knew it was imminent.

Then she knew nothing at all.

***

Three months later…

"Tell me every detail," Doctor Andrews said. "One more time."

Carmen took a deep breath and gazed out of the window, down at the streets she used to wander relentlessly. How she wished she could walk them now. How she wished she could be alone once more. Unseen and avoided by everyone.

"It happens in Texas, a man alone with several large guns, he attacks a university, he wears camouflage gear," Carmen said.

"Which University?"

"I don't know. A sign said that there was some kind of open event, at seven tonight it said."

"Right, okay. What kind of event?"

"I don't know, I'm sorry. I didn't see."

Doctor Andrews tapped his pen. He always wrote her predictions down on crisp white paper. It didn't matter to him that everything was recorded on tape and on cameras, which were poured over for hours by a team of experts. He still wanted his own notes.

"You must try harder, Carmen," Doctor Andrews frowned. "Texas is a big place."

Carmen knew that.

She was trying as hard as she possibly could. She had been since she met the psychiatrist.

After her accident, and while she was in the hospital, there were worries over her mental health. Her insistence that she could see future events. A day later, in bed and with her leg in plaster, in walked Doctor Susanna Blake.

Tall, dark-haired, and with keen, clever eyes, Carmen had told her everything. The plane crash, the tall, suited man, the cruise ship, the earthquake.

Even her latest visions, the ones put into her mind as she slept. Dreams of a huge pile-up on the M1, a coach crash in Italy, the volcano eruption, and the attack on a British army base.

Of course, Susanna called her rantings delusions, fantasies, and prescribed several pills. Until the ocean liner The Genevieve suffered a massive engine malfunction, exploded, and sank very quickly near Greece.

A coincidence, Doctor Blake had called the event. Just a coincidence.

Until an earthquake almost destroyed downtown L.A.

Events had happened quickly after that.

Carmen had been moved to what they called The Facility. She knew the building was in London central; she recognized the streets and shops far below her. Even though her leg was healed, she wasn't allowed to leave.

No. She was too much of a valuable asset according to the secretive team around her.

Every day, a woman arrived to ask her what she would like to eat. What she would like to wear. Those were her only choices in life.

She had two hours allotted to her for personal time. Which meant bathing, exercise, and eating. For the other twenty-two hours a day, Carmen was given powerful sedatives and sleeping pills. She was only valuable for her dreams, for the events she could see in her sleep.

As soon as she awoke from her many nightmares, Doctor Andrews, or sometimes other doctors, would appear and take notes.

Then she would be forced to sleep again.

Cameras circled the room. The door was locked; the windows reinforced with thick glass and bars.

No way out.

Carmen finally had her comfortable bed, her regular meals, her walls, and her safety.

Her brain itched and felt full of grey mist. She longed to be free, let loose from her gilded, pretty cage.

This is what it's like to go slowly insane.

Doctor Andrews handed her a pot with two tablets inside. She nodded and swallowed. If she refused, she would be forced. It had happened before, several times. He took her blood pressure and nodded.

"Back to sleep then," he said.

Carmen rose and crossed the room to the comfortable bed. Even with exercise once a day, she wondered if her muscles were failing. She felt weak and fatigued, unhinged from too much sleep. Confused and half-delirious.

"Can I have an extra hour awake tomorrow?" She asked.

"We'll see," he replied. A parent's answer to a child, which really meant no.

Carmen knew her predictions were coming true. She had been told repeatedly.

What she didn't know was if they, whoever *they* really were, were trying to prevent them.

She had no access to the news and no one would ever tell her. Despite her desperation and her pleading.

"Sleep well," Doctor Andrews said and left. Heavy locks locking her in sounded.

The pills were already working, sleep and dreams were rushing headlong towards her.

An escape from the room, yes. An escape from the warm bed she had craved, and escape from the walls she had once yearned for. But an escape into new terrors and frightening situations she could only watch.

A new circle of hell for her. A never-ending state of horror. The hope she had always carried had long ago left her.

Still, she was helping people, and that mattered to her a great deal.

She closed her eyes to dream. Her last image before she slept was the tall suited man standing in the corner, observing, watching, unseen by the many cameras.

Seeing the future was not a blessing after all, but a curse. At least, it was for her.

Carmen slept. Carmen dreamed...

Imagine if you will, the death of yourself or a loved one, avoided by the words of a modern-day prophet.

Carmen Russel, age thirty-five. A lonely woman, a calm and loving soul.

Needed desperately by the society she adored.

Dreamer, prophet, cursed with visions of the future.

The saver of lives. The hero no one ever heard of.

Trapped within four walls and one roof. Trapped within her bed and within her mind. Visions planted.

A warning given to one, for the benefit of all. To save the many.

Prophecies once written on a subway wall...

SEARCH FOR ANSWERS

For your thought and entertainment.

Witness, Mr. William Meadows. A lonely, somewhat arrogant man. An individual on a solitary quest for internet fame. A man who craves to be seen and one who yearns to be heard.

A man on a quiet vacation, whose search for proof and answers, might lead him to the most terrible of truths.

There are more things in heaven and earth, or so they say.

We do not know what we do not know, and we do not know that we do not know.

An open mind is needed.

Are we alone? No, we have never been alone…

Destination. Unimaginable.

William Meadows wanted to be famous in his chosen field of truth-seeking.

He prided himself on being an intelligent man. One with a mind far greater than those around him.

In truth, he quite wrongly viewed his I.Q. as superior.

William, or Will as he liked to be called, had spent the majority of his adult life searching for answers.

Answers to the only question he believed might be relevant to the world. Are we being visited by extraterrestrial intelligences?

He knew the answer had to be yes, of course, they were visiting, but he wanted proof, something tangible, and he needed to be the one to find it.

His quest had long since become a personal obsession.

Will studied estimated flight patterns of UFOs, newly released and heavily redacted government files, abduction reports, downed unknown aircraft rumors, and missing person reports. He came to the only conclusion he was able, that alien entities were taking people. Simply snatching human beings straight out of national parks as they hiked or hunted, vacationed, or wandered.

Sometimes a person came back, sometimes they did not.

He believed the extraterrestrials were friends and not foes. His conclusion being that the missing had chosen to leave earth behind and go off with their space brothers and sisters.

Maybe they were taken to live on new planets? Planets with glorious skies and peaceful races. Planets with no wars, no hunger, and no poverty or disease.

Will believed a cover-up was firmly in place, authorized by members of a secret, sinister cabal hidden inside the world's government.

Will's set beliefs, his refusal to consider anything else as relevant or important, his lack of family and friends, might well have contributed to how he found himself: somewhere inside a large national park, hanging upside down, certain death was upon him.

A conclusion he made, far, far too late.

***

Will parked his old rattling car in the designated parking area, pleased to find there were not as many cars as he expected.

Which most certainly meant fewer people.

He grinned widely and climbed out of his vehicle, intent on emptying his trunk. He breathed in the crisp fresh air, deep breaths to fill his lungs, and stretched.

A brief swell of happiness began to swirl inside of him.

Will had not taken a real vacation in years. The only breaks from work he ever took were spent in his small apartment fighting zombies or gruesome aliens in online battles.

Then there was his YouTube channel, the channel Will worked so very hard on and was proud of but one that still only had twenty-two subscribers.

No one wanted to hear his theories, or his *truths,* as Will called them. YouTube channels were a popularity contest as far as he was concerned, and he was not popular enough. Not even close.

"This is perfect!" he mumbled to himself, thoroughly pleased by his genius idea to combine a vacation with research. For him, the next seven days would be a chance to think, to reassess his life, and investigate the recent disappearances in the rugged wilderness at the very same time.

Will was intending to look for scorch marks, perhaps even trace radiation from a landed spacecraft he might pick up on with his new Geiger counter, one he brought straight from eBay.

Will lugged his backpack from the car and struggled to get it on firmly and stay upright.

I feel like a turtle! He thought and chuckled to himself. His pack contained food, a water purifier, a tent, a sleeping bag, cooking equipment, and the most important thing, his video camera.

He intended to solve the mysteries of the national park, capture UFO footage and upload the lot to please his twenty-two fans.

I'll have one thousand and twenty-two soon! No, two thousand or more. Finally, people will notice me!

Will liked to think positively, needed his cleverness and determination to be recognized.

Back in his small apartment, crammed in next to his noisy neighbors, life had begun to take its toll.

At age fifty, his lack of success in finding a partner, a new job, fans, and proof of his theory had led him to break down on a live stream and sob. Will saw that no one was actually watching anyway, and so he'd sat and cried, emptied his mind of upset, and vowed to keep trying, more determined than ever.

This is going to be my greatest adventure! I'll be famous!

Will was not wrong.

He grinned and locked his car, turned to face the rugged trail. He felt as if he were leaving one world behind for another. From a bustling city to the quiet, noble serenity of nature. Thick luscious trees stood facing him, lined up soldier-like, and formed a border. A transition line between two worlds.

Walking quickly, eagerly, Will climbed the jagged steps. He switched his camera on and aimed it into the depths of the national park.

"My vacation and the search for answers start now!" He spoke. "And I have a good feeling about this!"

He stepped into the woods. Into his new rugged world.

"Now, I have a map I printed out from the internet. On it are the locations where just some of the missing were last seen according to important online sources."

By important sources, he meant his own Facebook group, one that boasted a whole five members.

As Will spoke to his camera, he imagined a large, envious audience watching as he captured the thick woodland around him. It occurred to him just how easily a person could become lost. The park stretched for many miles, with caves spread around and nestled like honeycombs.

Still, Will knew best. He knew he wouldn't become lost. No, he had two compasses and a flare gun lodged inside his pack. He wasn't taking any chances.

To save power, he turned his camera off and concentrated on walking. In his mind, he imagined himself as an internet sensation, maybe even with a guest appearance on one of the big UFO documentary shows. In demand and sought after for his expert opinions, and finally recognized for his bravery and genius. Will, a lone crusader, relentless in his search, fearless and remarkable.

After only two hours, Will's legs began to tire. He cursed himself for his lack of fitness and sat to rest on a large boulder. He consulted his map and concentrated.

Wait, is this map upside down?

"Good morning!" A sudden voice made him jolt.

Two men were coming towards him, a big slobbery dog between them. Both were dressed in hiking gear.

"Hi!" Will waved and immediately felt awkward. Social interaction was not something he was particularly good at.

"I'm on vacation! I didn't expect to see anyone," he grinned.

"Why not? You're right near the entrance." The two men chuckled.

Will blushed furiously. He thought he had walked for miles already. He gazed around and shrugged. To him, everything looked the same. Understanding dawned.

I've walked in a circle!

"That way," the taller of the two men said, and pointed. "And keep goin'."

"Thanks," Will mumbled. He dropped his pack and rummaged for his compass, decided to follow that and not the map.

Quickly, he scurried away. The laughter of the men made his face turn redder.

Okay, okay. So I made a mistake, so what? It won't happen again.

Will gulped from his water bottle as he walked and went off the set trail. He decided to push himself harder, break the pain barrier he'd heard other people talk about. Sweat dripped down his back, his shoulders burned. Still, he pushed on. He wound through clusters of trees, slid down slopes, hiked up, and back down.

After three hours, he stopped and dropped his pack.

He was near water. A quiet stream two feet across with cool water that looked fairly clear.

I'll camp here. This is perfect.

Around him, no one. Only tree after tree surrounded him, only broken up by thick spiky bushes.

Pleased with himself and his adventure, he set up his tent on the only flat ground he could find and set his camera up.

"My first night of vacation! In the wilderness, I'm hoping to see UFOs or orbs, anything unusual, and hopefully something unique for you guys!"

He lay his camera down and grinned. He felt free and proud of himself. He expected to feel lonely, but really, he was more than used to that feeling.

He looked forward to the night ahead. He ate quickly and lay down in his tent. He aimed to stay awake all night and grab a couple of hour's sleep while it was still light. He really did feel exhausted. Weary all the way into his bones, a happy kind of tired, as if he had achieved something amazing.

This is the best vacation ever.

Will smiled as he slept.

***

He awoke to thick darkness. Impenetrable to his vision. For a few seconds, he panicked wildly and forgot where he was entirely.

The realization came crashing back. He laughed and wiped his face, felt for his torch, and clicked it on. Light surrounded him and chased away the night.

I should have built a fire pit.

Will had viewed a few survivalist videos and convinced himself he didn't need to practice techniques—it all looked easy enough. Besides, he had matches. He was going to cheat.

He climbed out of his tent, back sore and legs aching.

The view over his head almost took his breath away. A fat full moon and stars. Stars shining more brightly than he'd ever seen before. Hundreds of them littered the sky. Beautiful constellations he failed to remember the names of.

Will enjoyed feeling so insignificant, so primitive as he gazed. He could only imagine the worlds and civilizations that he knew must be out there and visiting earth.

Wait, one moved. A star flashed once and made its way slowly across the night sky.

Satellite, or space station?

He gasped loudly as the small light zoomed off at an impossibly high speed.

He fumbled for his camera, too late.

"Idiot!" He cursed himself. "That clip would have had hundreds of views!"

Disappointment washed over him. Will did not like feeling so useless. He forced his mind to think on the bright side.

The light will come back, I'll wait all night if I have to. Aliens come here, I know it.

He pulled his sleeping bag out of his tent and sat quietly, camera on, and waited.

Silence engulfed him. Thick, absolute silence.

Will found he needed the quiet. No office noise, no loud neighbors, no sirens, no alarms. Just peace.

He lay back and watched the sky, searched and wondered.

Why are aliens taking us?

Will knew all the theories, had researched them extensively. Breeding, genetic manipulation, for the population of other planets, for work, for sport, and so on. He knew that sometimes people were abducted and returned. He knew of several famous cases, still, his greatest desire was to learn the why. He believed he knew all about the who and how, aliens, in their universe traveling ships. The Grays and Nordics, he was certain.

Will believed the government had a deal with them. Like some whistleblowers claimed.

If that's the case, then underground bases must be real. Dulce too and ...

The sound of a branch snapping made Will jerk upright.

Must be an animal?

Will knew cryptids had been seen in the park he was in and reported. For all his belief in aliens, he had none in Bigfoot or any other strange and elusive creatures.

Still, he worried about wild animals, ones that may attack him, a bear or even a mountain lion.

He listened out hard for further sounds, grabbed his camera just in case.

Will's mouth fell open, his stomach plummeted as he caught sight of a small light flitting through the trees.

Oh my gosh, an orb!

Excitement built as he pressed record and captured the movement of the circular light. The orb was light blue; it danced and sailed as if controlled by an intelligence. Will watched in absolute wonder, his mind emptied of all thoughts.

The orb juddered, blinked twice, and vanished.

Do they know I'm here? Have they seen me?

Without warning, a woman came stumbling out of the tree line and headed straight towards him. Will's heart stuttered at the sight of her.

Not an orb, a torch!

He aimed his own light at her, almost cried out with fear. The front of her clothing was blood-drenched, her hair and face too. Her expression was one of sheer panic.

"Run," she gasped. "Run! They're coming."

Will had never experienced such shock, such terror, never felt such a coldness inside himself, such a brutal primal fear.

"Wh… What!" He yelled and ran back and forth uselessly, unable to process the woman's warning.

The woman pounded past him and left him standing alone, open-mouthed and afraid. She crossed the stream in a couple of leaps, raced off, and out of sight. A shrill scream sounded from her direction.

Will dropped to a crouch, confused, terrified.

Who's coming? What's coming!

Adrenaline coursed through him, his heart thudded and filled his head with sound and white noise.

A roar burst from the treeline, a deep noise with low threatening tones of fury.

Will rolled until he felt shielded by a boulder.

He did not know if he should run or hide, cower or find bravery inside.

He found fear had overridden his need for truth, his need to prove his worth.

It dawned on him for the first time that he should never have gone looking for something he might actually find.

A shape emerged from the trees, a figure. Tall and wide, fur-covered and furious.

Oh my...

Will stumbled backward. His mind froze, all thoughts failed. He landed in the water and scrambled up. Every atom of his body told him to run away as fast as he could.

Will did just that.

He ran into the woods, screaming a wretched wail of fear.

His feet pounded the hard ground. He veered around trees and fallen logs. Frantically, he spun, searching for whatever it was he'd seen, sure it must be close behind him. He felt his body impact a tree. He hit the ground, his skull bounced painfully. He lay on his back, dazed.

Vaguely, Will realized blood was flowing from his head. Above the tree canopy, bright lights formed a circle and slowly descended. He could smell sulfur and rot.

"Help," he croaked before he passed out.

***

Will opened a single eye, unsure of where he was, for a moment, unsure of even who he was. Only thick darkness drew tightly around him.

A deep smell of decay hit his senses, dampness and nastiness engulfed him.

He tested his mouth, tried to speak. Nothing. His tongue felt too dry to form words, and his head thudded painfully.

He vomited. Hot liquid rushed down his face and into his hair. It was then that Will realized he was hanging upside down. He thrashed wildly, and for the first time, felt severe bindings around his ankles.

Panic took hold fast and sharp. He wailed in disbelief, terror, and despair.

Where am I? What's happening?!

He let off a piercing scream of fright.

"Shut up!" A man's deep voice spoke. "You'll have them things storming in here!"

The voice echoed. As if they were underground somehow. Will could hear the steady drip, drip, drip of water, and felt the coldness of the damp.

He blinked rapidly, tried hard to focus.

"Who's there?" He managed to croak.

He felt like a fish on the end of a rod, flapping uselessly around.

"Get me down," he added.

"Can't," the voice replied. "I'm stuck. We all are. We were camping. They took us."

"Where are we? Where am I? Who took us?"

Will's mind immediately blamed humans. A group of inbred cannibals, maybe? Like in those movies he once watched. Or could it be human trafficking?

Either option was terrifying.

Somewhere off in the distance came the sharp sound of metal clanging, joined with guttural voices talking in a language he couldn't place.

Wait! Hold on, have I been…

"Are we abductees!" Will gasped. "Aliens!"

"Shhh!" said the voice. "Stay still!"

A door opened, light flooded in. Will squinted and saw figures dressed in a light silver material head towards him. Around him hung several people, all upside down. Most were unconscious from what he could tell. One seemed to be the woman who had fled past him.

Cold terror seeped into him as comprehension dawned. He was a prisoner and the figures were grays. Stereotypical gray aliens from abduction lore. A group of six surrounded him as he jerked and swung in his ankle bindings.

Large unblinking eyes glared at him, emotionless faces stared. Large heads with small thin bodies.

"Let me go, please," Will begged. "Please!"

One reached out and poked him with a slender finger that sent him swinging gently. Another jabbed him with a sharp, metallic object. Black spots burst across his vision as pain erupted inside him.

Keep calm. They'll send me back. Just cooperate. I know what they do, I read all about it. I'll talk about this, this will make me famous.

Sounds rang out, a high-pitched beep followed by a hiss. Will fell to the hard ground. He instinctively tried to flip over, tried to scramble up on his knees. One of the grays grabbed his ankles and yanked.

NO! This isn't what happens to abductees in books!

He screamed as he was dragged across the floor. Begged and pleaded as the gray pulled him along. His fingers tried to clutch the ground, his body scraped across stone and sharp rocks.

This is a cave, not a spaceship.

He panicked, wiggled frantically, and felt a blow to the back of his head, felt pain explode, and then nothing at all.

***

As he came to, again, a face stared at him, inches away from his own. He jolted in horror at the monstrous creature. The creature, in turn, sniffed him deeply and licked its twisted lips. Its breath smelt so rancid, Will almost choked on the fumes.

Eyes of bright yellow assessed him, curious, intelligent eyes. An obscene mouth opened and revealed several layers of sharp, brutal teeth. The creature stepped back, studied him thoughtfully. It stood at least seven feet in height, a powerful lithe body, fur-covered and fierce.

Will found he could not think, could not move. Body and mind were frozen in synchronicity.

A sharp pain in his head, a reminder of his injury, broke his stillness. He opened his mouth to scream. The creature mimicked him and laughed.

Will seemed to be in a large room, along with the creature. White walls, ones far too white and bright surrounded him.

Before his eyes, the strange creature melted away, like a hologram breaking apart. Will watched in amazement as the creature gave way to a small, gray alien. Before he could blink, the gray shuddered, rippled, and became a tall, quite beautiful nordic woman.

"But…" Will gasped.

The nordic woman switched and became a reptilian entity. A long tongue flicked out and licked the air. The reptilian hissed and shifted into a giant, thin praying mantis, complete with translucent wings.

Will's mind pinged apart at the edges. The figure moved again, diminished in size, and settled on one impossible shape.

A thing from nightmares stood before him, with taloned feet and gargoyle-faced features. Long arms with brutal claws. It snarled savagely and leaped forward. Two small wings spread out behind it. Its skin appeared leathery, scaled.

It looks like… a demon!

Will had seen the image of such a thing before, in old books of ancient history and in plenty of horror movies.

"NO!" He instinctively cried. He tried to throw his arms up, quickly understanding that more binding held him firmly in place.

The thing jumped on his chest with a heavy thud.

A bombardment of images hit Will. Knowledge of the impossible. Not aliens at all, never extraterrestrial. But a sinister force, existing for eons, owning and treating humankind as nothing more than cattle. Tricksters and illusionists.

An ancient evil using humans as playthings.

An abhorrent race gifting themselves different names over the centuries, personas to hide their crimes. From ancient gods to demons. From demonic nightmares to folklore creatures, from folklore into aliens.

There were many of them, countless. A legion, an army.

Entities with a thousand changing masks, a thousand names, and all were disguises. Snatching people over centuries, and for what?

Will had his answers. Will finally knew the truth.

The knowledge snapped his last piece of sanity. He screamed wildly in desperation. Buckled in hopelessness.

He was food. But not his flesh, no, not his skin and bone.

The thing, the evil entity, held him in position and sucked, fed.

White-hot agony tore through Will. He felt himself being shredded apart and brutally so. Pulled apart at the seams.

His essence, his soul, consciousness, the thing that made him, *him*, was ripped from his body, out of his own mouth, and devoured by the nightmarish creature, gulped and swallowed.

His heart jerked and shuddered. Stopped entirely.

Will, dead. No, more than dead, ceased to exist. Nothing more than an irrelevant carcass and one who once knew the terrifying truth.

***

Will Meadows yearned to be famous in his chosen field of truth-seeking.

News of his disappearance on his long-overdue vacation spread. He became one of many to vanish inside the national park and one of six separate individuals to vanish in just one single night.

His smashed camera and camping equipment were found by search and rescue teams, half-hidden among boulders by the water. One single shoe was found by rescue dogs in the woodland before the trail turned cold.

Popular YouTube channels talked about Will. A man on a search for answers, and on vacation no less, was missing without a trace, like so many others.

In his absence, many found, liked, and subscribed to his channel, in memory of him, in solidarity.

Some assumed Will had given up on life, some assumed Will had been taken or fallen prey to an animal attack or unfortunate accident.

All hoped he had at least found his answers, wherever he was…

Mr. William Meadows.

A sole man on a search for answers. A man who discovered the incomprehensible truth far too late.

A man who does not exist anymore.

Be wary.

Sometimes, when peering into darkness and realms unseen, something else may be peering straight back.

The truth may set you free, but first, it may frighten you to death…

MIRROR DARKLY

Narcissism.

A term originating from Greek mythology, wherein a young man named Narcissus fell in love with his own beautiful reflection.

The pursuit of gratification via vanity. Egotistical admiration of oneself.

Adoration of the self.

While balance is sought by most, as always, the scales tip. One might have no care at all for their own appearance, one might have some, while another may care far too much.

Witness Miss. Leah Chambers, a young woman with a bleak, most twisted heart, and owner of a beautiful face.

The receiver of a most strange gift.

How far is too far?

Leah Chambers, a young woman who will do anything for beauty...

Leah stares at herself in one of her many mirrors. She gazes a hundred times a day, sometimes even a thousand. At times, she even becomes lost in her own image, enthralled by her features, captivated, and enraptured.

She adores her own reflection, admires her own beauty, her face is her obsession.

Although, her looks are all based on illusion and carefully constructed chaos, nothing more than lies twisted together to form a mask of sorts.

She views her elegant appearance as a special form of art.

The altered and sculpted shape of her nose, perfect. The arch of her colored brows, the fullness of her injected lips. The smoothness of her skin, no blemishes or wrinkles, and no lines, thanks to Botox and fillers. Her eyelash extensions, full of carefully applied mascara, are designed to look vivid at every angle.

Her hair is lush and full, all brown colors mixed together to create a beautiful shimmer effect. The hair itself is all fake extensions, hair she got for free for advertising a certain brand.

She once read online that the company buys real human hair, cheaply, from women living in poverty. Leah doesn't care where the hair came from. She only cares about what it looks like on her.

To her, the suffering of others is irrelevant and worth no thought in her callous mind.

Since she was a child, people have constantly told her how pretty she is, how beautiful. How doll-like with her wavy hair and porcelain smooth skin. Leah laps up the attention as if it is essential to life, and for her, it is.

Perfect on the outside, maybe so. But inside? Inside lives a hollowness, a place where kindness should have made a home. No warmth has a place in her heart, no love for anything but her own reflection exists.

***

Years before, Leah quickly learned how to use her looks to her advantage. A certain look she perfected made those around her give in to her demands. A few tears added, could command the coldest of hearts. A pout could ensure an extension of an exam. The flutter of her eyelashes would cause another to write her exam paper for her. A temper tantrum was inevitable if she didn't get her own way. She wanted to be the center of everyone's world and felt she deserved to have such a place.

Those around her became her enablers, simply to buy themselves peace from her demands. It was the fuel to push her further.

Selfishness, jealousy, narcissism, arrogance, and, of course, vanity, became her own personal dark traits and each one only grew in size and depth.

Fame. Absolute fame is what she always sought.

***

Now, she grabs her phone, ensures the light is perfect, and takes a few selfies, checks them, chooses one, adds filters, and uploads the results.

Her personal congregation, her followers react immediately. She is envied online, adored, and admired.

Others see a kind, popular, vibrant girl. The camera distorts the truth so elegantly.

She is a fake girl with a life built purely on lies, hidden behind clever illusions.

Only two hundred and six likes! She thinks. That can't be right!

The number isn't good enough. Nowhere near, actually. A feeling of pain bursts across her chest, the unknown emotion of feeling so insignificant and small. She hates the pain such a thing brings.

Jealousy plagues her, a new girl is after her crown. She sees her rival's profile: more friends, more followers, more likes, more sponsors, more carefully crafted beauty.

For Leah, this won't do at all.

She crosses her room to her cosmetic-covered dressing table, intent on creating a new look for herself, one that can be amplified by clever filters. She ties her hair back, removes her current make-up.

The face that stares back at her is her nemesis and one she cannot, no, will not accept. She cannot stand to be anything less than perfect, will not accept herself as less.

Her bare face is beautiful, not perfect, no, but true. Real and genuine. All she sees is ugliness. She does not realize, the ugliness comes from inside, not out.

She is a beauty trickster, a mimic. Her prettiness is designed and applied. Clever tricks, filters, and nothing more.

She fools others. Encourages them to understand and agree with her view that looks are more important than anything, except maybe money. Leah loves money too, although she won't lift a finger to earn her own.

Quickly she covers her small amount of acne and blotches until her skin appears flawless. She applies her cosmetics, layer after layer.

With her mask firmly in place, she styles her hair, changes her clothes, and races out into her parent's small backyard.

There, she lays on the grass, spends an hour making sure her hair is spread out behind her without a single strand out of place.

She applies filters and takes selfie after selfie, laying in the cool grass. The image does not at all resemble real life.

Leah is chasing the perfect shot. The one that might award her a new sponsor with enough money to keep her parents off her back.

She believes she shouldn't have to work, shouldn't have to have a job. Not with a face and skills like her own.

She uploads the image, closes her eyes, and waits. There. Over six hundred likes, and all it took was a little foolery and magic.

Hours later, a message pops up on her account. A new sponsor.

'Would you like to help advertise our new product? We are looking for beautiful women like yourself. Click for details.'

Leah clicks. She follows links and types in her information. As far as she is concerned, she has outdone her rival, and that is all she truly cares about.

***

Two days later, a new package arrives for her. She is used to pretty boxes being delivered, usually filled with goodies and free make-up to try, clothes to wear and advertise, and special diet drinks she pretends she enjoys but pours away.

Inside the pink box, tucked under layers of bright pink tissue, sits a handheld mirror.

It's pretty in a dark, gothic kind of way, with intricate carvings around the edges, images of roses and flowers. The mirror itself is black. A black surface with no reflection.

Leah laughs, wondering if the manufacturer has made an error. She holds the mirror up to the light, feeling confusion and uncertainty. She shrugs. So what if it's faulty? The company is paying her. She intends to use the money for more essential hair extensions.

I'll just pretend I love it. It's what I do after all.

She runs upstairs, showers, and applies her multiple layers of cosmetics. I'll make a video, and take some selfies too.

A message pings on her phone from her best friend Eve. A party that same night. Is she going?

No. Leah can't be in control of how she looks at a party. One badly angled photograph could destroy her. But then again, maybe if

70

she arrives early, takes selfies with her friend, and leaves, she might be seen as more popular online? It might bring her more followers and even more envy. She doesn't mind using people, she thrives on such a thing.

She types back yes and opens her laptop, ready to record her video. The lighting is all wrong in her bedroom. She's asked her parents a thousand times for new curtains and they just won't listen.

Leah believes they are both unfair to her. She is their only child, and she believes she should be adored and spoiled. So what if her mother has to work extra hours to make ends meet? So what if her father has health problems? Those aren't Leah's problems.

She hangs a blanket from the curtain pole, makes sure it's hidden from sight, and rearranges her hair. It has to be perfect, after all.

Wow, I look so beautiful!

Sometimes, the sight of her own appearance stuns her. She tilts her head, admires all angles. Her contouring technique is remarkable and she knows it.

Her father told her she could be a great make-up artist. Leah has no desire to make other people look beautiful, only herself. She intends to marry a rich man and wear her layers of make-up to bed each night. She doesn't think her ideas are ridiculous.

I only need to be seen by the right set of eyes. That's all. Who could fail to fall in love with me?! I'm glorious!

She arranges her posture, straightens up, and presses record. She does not do live streams, she likes to edit too much.

She watches her own videos repeatedly until she is sure they are flawless.

"Hi, guys!" Leah speaks in a fake voice too. Upbeat and happy, two things she is not.

"I have something beautiful to show you and it's super gorgeous! I just know you'll all want one!"

She makes eye contact with the camera, blinks, and throws her hair over her shoulder. She adds a wide smile.

"This is my gift! I'm so, so happy with it. What do you think?"

She lifts the mirror and shows it, turns it, and tries to show every angle.

"I think this is…"

She stops. That dark reflection in the glass ripples, the black mirror shimmers. Movement catches her eye. She squints, forgetting the camera is on her and gazes.

Light appears. A shape forms from the depths of the blackness. A human figure draped in what she thinks are torn rags.

"What is this!" she gasps. A prank, a gimmick, and a cruel one at that. It has to be.

She turns the mirror over, examines it closely.

Some kind of recording inside?

She gazes back at the glossy surface, watches as the figure floats towards her. Mist spirals around beside it, half wrapping it in darkness.

Entranced, she stares.

A face appears. Old and lined, the face of a gruesome hag. One pure white eye blinks at her before its mouth opens and roars, showing jagged, rotten teeth. There is no sound, only the noise of static plays in Leah's mind.

The scene switches. She sees the reflection of a girl's face, a girl just like herself only ruined.

Fish hooks penetrate skin and nerve, blood drips slowly, weeps, as each one is yanked viciously by unseen hands. One eye has been sewn shut, with thick barbed wire. The girl has no nose, only a hollow hole, gore-filled, and riddled with crawling maggots. Her lips are pulled back in a sneer, a fat black tongue lolls out, flies burst from her mouth.

Leah can smell rot and decay. Can feel fear rising inside of her.

"This is disgusting!" She yells and throws the mirror.

Her breathing is rapid, uneven. Terror and disbelief claw at her heart.

"How can?… How is…"

For Leah, she has seen the impossible come to life.

The girl in the mirror was herself and she knew it. That is how she would look if her inside self became her surface self. Quickly, she jumps up and stamps on the mirror, and pushes her thoughts away.

The satisfying break of glass fills the room. One single maggot appears, makes an exit from the mirror, and tries to crawl away. Flies, big fat flies follow it.

Leah screams.

***

"It was just a cruel prank Darling," her mother soothes her. "There must have been a camera inside. They can make them tiny these days, can't they?"

Leah won't listen, refuses.

She cannot stop the fear rising inside of her, the fright. The old hag, the girl, it was her.

That's who I am on the inside, all rotten. Oh, fuck it, who cares who I am deep down!

"Leave me alone," Leah snaps. "You're useless. Always so useless!"

She cannot help herself. She has never once tried to be kind.

Her mother sighs and cleans up the glass, knowing full well her daughter will not clean up after herself. She closes the bedroom door with a sad, quiet click, visibly upset.

Leah turns over in her bed, more tears flow. She has never cried so much in her life. How will she take selfies with such red sore eyes? How will she go to the party? And get more followers to beat her rival? She needs a bigger audience.

Wait. Her rival.

What if she did this?!

Leah scrambles up, rummages for her phone. The girl has posted a photo of herself outdoors, sitting among flowers with a single rose in her hair. The image has thousands of likes.

This isn't fair. I'm more beautiful than her. I am! That should be me.

A message pings, from her friend Eve, *'What time shall I pick you up?'* it says.

'Fuck off and leave me alone,' Leah types back.

She always talks that way to people. Besides, she thinks Eve is ugly. She doesn't want selfies with her. She won't get the likes she needs that way unless they are from pity.

A sharp pain in her head makes her gasp. As quickly as it arrives, it's gone again, then back, gone, back, until a rapid pulsing sensation begins to occur.

Leah stumbles out of bed and lands on her bedroom floor. It feels to her as if the carpet is undulating. As if the room is spinning. She can't think straight, thoughts collide and shatter. Bright vivid spots burst across her vision until the world itself turns briefly black.

When she awakes, the pain is gone. Vanished.

The repercussions have left Leah with an idea. An idea that is not her own.

Half in a daze, and not at all sure of her destination, she walks downstairs and out into the garage. She feels dizzy, weak. As if she is in a dream state.

Her make-up is smeared, her hair is wild. Still, for the first time in her life, she has forgotten to care. She finds what she needs among her father's tools and boxes and heads back upstairs.

A black pit of despair is twisting around inside of her. She feels almost certain, no, positive, that what she intends to do is the right thing. Her new idea seems to make perfect sense. She wonders why she hasn't thought of it before, it seems so obvious.

Carefully, she sits at her dressing table. She blinks and breathes, moves, and sighs. All tangled thoughts in her mind. All will is absent.

She switches on her laptop and prepares for a live stream. Her movements are jerky, puppet-like. A hypnotic state, both aware and yet not.

She is live. She waits for an audience. They soon appear, slowly at first, until clusters arrive, word spreads.

She unclenches her fist, reveals the fish hooks taken from her father's tackle box.

As viewers watch her, she pinches her face and pierces her skin.

The sharp metal penetrates her cheek. Leah does not cry out as blood springs to the surface, does not grimace or feel a thing. Her skin is tougher than she expected. She has to push hard to get the metal inside and back out.

Next, she pierces her bottom lip, forcing the metal in and through. An eyelid next, that one goes in smoothly, easily. Blood drips down her face, into her eye. She doesn't notice.

She doesn't see the comments from her viewers flooding the screen, the horror, the outrage, the shock, the cruel laughter, the vile encouragement.

She takes scissors firmly in her hands and cuts off her hair, starting as close to her scalp as she can, hack, hack, cut, cut. Off it falls onto her carpet.

Next comes a jagged knife, one kept for gutting fish. She uses the brutal edges to slice off a portion of her nose, the very tip. She grips tightly and cuts until the cartilage and bone are exposed for all to see.

As an afterthought, she slices the flesh of her chest and arms. Deep savage cuts that open wide.

A hammer.

She picks up the solid weight and tests it. Downstairs, a phone starts to ring. The high-pitched shrill sounds like a warning. A brief glance at the screen tells her thousands of people are watching her, thousands and thousands. The biggest audience she's ever had.

Somewhere inside, in the remnants of herself, she is pleased, proud of herself.

As footsteps come pounding up the stairs, she smashes herself in the face with the hammer.

Teeth splinter and crack, an explosion of blood erupts. She spits out several teeth as her bedroom door flies open and her father wrestles her to the floor.

***

Leah tried to tell the doctors that the black mirror made her do it. She tried to tell them that the mirror revealed to her, her true self. The one hid beneath the surface of the mask she applied and wore each day.

They tell her *No, it wasn't the mirror*. They say her mind is sick.

She is not allowed the internet. She is not allowed her phone.

Instead, she lays in a small room with white walls and takes pills that make her feel sick or as if she is floating.

Bandages are wrapped around her face, stitches dig in, her teeth are missing. Sometimes her parents come to see her. They sit on each side of the bed and hold her hands. No one speaks. No one knows what to say. Leah wonders why they still love her when she has been so cruel.

Outside, the sun shines. She has forgotten what being outside feels like. She only knows stale air and the smell of antiseptic.

One day Eve arrives to see her. She brings magazines and drinks of cold diet coke.

Leah wonders why her friend wants to know her, why she still cares after the way she has always treated her.

"I'm sorry," Leah tries to say. It's hard for her to talk, hard to form the words inside her broken mouth.

Eve shrugs and stays. She sits down and reads magazine articles out loud to her friend.

Leah realizes she is surrounded by good people, real people. People that are so very unlike herself.

Out of her one good eye, she watches her friend, listens.

"Although the video has been deleted by the server, it was copied and shared on multiple social media sites. The graphic live stream shows the breakdown of well-known and liked influencer, Leah Chambers."

That's me! It's about me!

Leah can't help but feel excited. The very worst aspects of herself listen intently.

"The video amassed ten thousand likes before it was removed, turning Leah from being just another influencer to an internet phenomenon. Well wishes and messages of support have poured in from all areas of the globe. We ask, just what is the price of fame and followers?"

"Am I famous?" Leah mumbles. "Am I?"

"Yes, you are. Everyone knows who you are now," Eve answers. "Everyone. Imagine the damage you could have done if I hadn't phoned your father."

Leah lets that fact sink in. Eve saved her but, finally, she made it. In the worst possible way, but she still made it. Her fans are sending well wishes. That must mean they want her back?

But I'm not beautiful anymore. I can't.

The idea of showing her face to the camera, to anyone, makes her blood run cold.

It's all over.

Who am I now? No one. Who cares who I am on the inside? That doesn't matter. Or does it?

Leah begins to cry out of her one good eye. She has no idea why she did what she did. She can only recall walking into the garage and then waking up in hospital. The rest is blank, scrubbed from her mind's hard drive. She has no idea of what she will do with her life or how she will ever be accepted.

A cold hard truth has slipped past Leah. Her looks are irrelevant.

"Don't cry," Eve says. "You only got what you deserve, after all."

"What?"

"I said. You only got what you deserve. I hope you liked your present, by the way. The cursed mirror, I hope you liked it. It gives a person what they deserve."

Eve stands up and laughs. She holds her phone up, angled so Leah, in her bed, is in the background and clicks, takes the shot.

"I've added, 'Visiting my sick friend.' That should get me plenty of likes. Anyway, see ya'!"

Cold, brutal despair and betrayal hit Leah so hard she jerks in her bed, pulls at her bandages, and wails.

She watches her friend leave, watches her enemy leave.

She screams about magic mirrors, wails about cursed mirrors until doctors rush in and sedate her into silence.

Scales tip, balance changes. The pursuit of one's own perfection, of one's own outer self, might be the path whose only destination leads to destruction.

Beware of pretty boxes, of gifts wrapped in pink. Beware black mirrors. Should you fall into its depths, you might never leave...

HOLES

Phobia. An extreme or often irrational aversion.

Paranoia. Unjustified suspicion or a deep mistrust of other people.

Sometimes, lines become blurred between clarity and chaos. Order for the spider is death for the captured fly.

The truth might lie somewhere inside an individual perspective. Can our own minds alter what we see and work hard against us? Or might the truth be hidden in plain sight? Or even somewhere in between?

Emotions, feelings, sense, instinct. Can they always be trusted?

Meet Lucy and Mike Taylor. A couple on a rural getaway, about to run into the improbable...

"I don't know what it is, Lucy," Mike told me as he crouched down. I heard the loud crack of his knees as he bent to examine the oddly shaped red blob. He didn't touch it, no, he poked it with a stick instead. It juddered slightly. As if it was made of a firm jelly substance.

"A mushroom?" I suggested. As if I'd even know.

What I *did* know was that I'd never seen a mushroom that size. The thing looked as big as a football.

"It might be a fungus, or maybe the tree has some kind of disease? A new one," Mike observed.

I gasped loudly, stifled a scream. I didn't like the sound of either idea, not one bit.

I didn't like the look of the blob, and I didn't want to camp in that area or anywhere near it.

The thing looked like a sea sponge to me, all made up of little holes and dark tunnels that made me feel sick. Somehow, it had grown into the shape of a mushroom and attached itself to a tree. A healthy-looking tree with thick, luscious bark. The blob looked entirely out of place, and deeply wrong.

Surely something like that belonged in deep, exotic oceans or coral reefs?

I put my hands over my eyes and peeked through my fingers. Looking at it made vomit rise in my mouth. Hole after hole, all hiding creeping, nasty slithering things, stared back and quivered gently.

I swallowed the burn of bile and gazed around to distract myself. Line after line of thick, gnarled trees surrounded us. We were standing in a small clearing of fairly bare ground.

The vast canopy of the thick woodland stretched over our heads and offered us cool shade away from the bright sun. The scenery was truly beautiful. I thought I might get bored looking at tree after tree, but after three days of hiking, I found I loved it and we still had four days left to enjoy. The air was crisp; the days were quiet. No one was around at all, not on the difficult trail we were on.

"Let's hike further," I said. "And find somewhere else to camp."

"No, Lucy, this is perfect here."

Mike was right, it was the only flat ground for miles, or at least, the only flat ground we'd come across, except, I had a problem.

"But… that thing looks… unnatural. Wrong. It's got holes, Mike. Holes."

Mike rolled his eyes and shook his head. After five years together and two years married, he was used to my ways, my phobias. People called them irrational, but to me, they were perfectly reasonable fears.

Still, the blob thing made me uneasy on a deep level I couldn't explain. That was always the case with me. Many things made me uneasy. I couldn't stand crowds, sudden movements, loud noises, things with holes in them, including cheese graters (don't ask) I hated tunnels, bridges, whistling sounds, and alarms. My fight-or-flight responses were locked onto permanent flight. My body and mind worked in opposites at times.

I needed routine. Structure. Ordinary days in order to feel relatively okay.

I liked the quiet, calm serenity of nature, which is why we always took our breaks in national parks. Being in nature meant I wouldn't panic, or at least, might panic less.

We'd chosen the Peak District, off the beaten track and far away from ramblers routes but close enough to tiny picturesque towns, just in case. In the three days we'd been out hiking, we'd only seen one couple. They offered us a friendly wave and kept on walking, eager for peace as much as we were.

"We'll be fine," Mike said and dropped his enormous pack.

"Fine, you can sleep near it. I'm not."

"Are you going to stay awake all night? Watching it?" He asked.

I decided not to answer. To say no would have been a lie.

I glanced at the blob and for a second, I thought I saw the thing move, thought I saw it almost breathe or shudder. I closed my eyes and concentrated.

Keep calm, it's only your imagination. I reminded myself of my therapists' mantra, the one I was supposed to practice and repeat.

But what if it did actually move? I dared to peek again. No. No movement.

"If the trees are infected, shouldn't we tell someone?" I said.

Mike shrugged and pulled at his beard. He did a lot, especially when he needed to think.

"It can't hurt to take a photograph," he said. We had our phones but no signals. I walked away and let Mike have the honors. I heard the click of his camera and began to open our pack.

Behind me, I could almost feel the thing watching me. I was sure of it, except, me being sure was something to be taken very lightly. I knew that.

Those holes, what's hiding down there? Is it alive?

The thought of that thing being alive and aware somehow made my head hiss. A wave of dizziness engulfed me.

Without warning, the thing suddenly seemed obscene, dangerous on a primal level I couldn't explain, sinister and evil. It had a plan, a plan to maim and kill, I was sure of it.

"Mike," I gasped. "I need to…"

It's all in my head. It's all in my head. Another mantra I told myself daily. The most useless one.

My hands started to shake. I fought my body's urge to run while my heart pounded erratically. Within seconds, Mike had his arms around me, half for comfort, half for keeping me firmly in place.

"Everything's fine," he repeated.

But no, everything was not fine. There was a thing on the tree, a growth that made me sick to my stomach and it was looking at me, right at me, judging.

It *felt* wrong, like things and situations often did. Like the time we were driving and I just absolutely knew the bridge we had to cross was going to collapse. Of course, it didn't, but still. Or like the time the crack on the ceiling in our flat was going to grow and cause the whole room to come crashing down on us while we slept. I thought if I watched it, if I stayed awake, it wouldn't dare to increase. But, the bridge was just a bridge, and a safe one at that. The crack was just a crack and nothing more. The thing was just an ordinary tree fungus, that was all.

I took deep breaths in and out, aware that sweat was pouring down my back.

I knew I had to stop this, had to find a way. What if Mike lost his patience with me? What if I ended up locked away in a mental health unit again? After the last time, I swore I wouldn't go back.

I waited for the fear to pass, as it always did, eventually.

"Sorry," I mumbled.

"It's okay, we'll keep walking, we'll camp someplace else."

There was always kindness in Mike's voice, depths, and textures of compassion. He was never annoyed by me. Even when I wouldn't go into his favorite restaurant for his birthday. I couldn't, you see, Mike had stepped on a crack in the pavement. It was as if he was asking for trouble.

I shook my head to loosen my thoughts.

You're safe. Absolutely safe.

"No, you're right, let's camp here," I said. I knocked on the hard ground four times for luck, then four more times, just to be sure.

Mike rummaged in his bag for a dirty shirt and launched it. It landed over the thing and covered it from view.

"There, all gone," he smiled.

I tried to smile back, but I could feel it assessing us, watching, and maybe even waiting.

***

I cooked some pasta over our tiny camping stove with our special fold-up saucepan. I had to cook, *had* to. The pasta had to be stirred one hundred and two times or it tasted funny. Mike set up our tent. Every so often, I glanced at the shirt covering the monstrosity.

What actually is it?

It was Mike who had gotten me into enjoying hiking and the outdoors. I didn't know all that much about nature. I couldn't name trees or plants. I knew what dandelion weeds were and thistles, nettles too. That was the sum of my knowledge.

If Mike can't identify it? Wait, what if it's...Oh my God, spores!

"Mike," I yelled. "What if it's toxic somehow, like mold? With spores!"

Spores terrified me. You could breathe them in and never know until they grew in your lungs and killed you dead. At least, that's what I believed.

"I don't think it's dangerous to us," he called back.

"You don't think? Or you're sure?"

I turned the stove off and waited. My skin felt itchy and hot. Just by being near the blob.

I looked at the shirt again, sure I saw the thing ripple underneath.

I rubbed my eyes and counted my fingers. Still nine. I lost one in an explosion, the incident that started my compulsions and rituals. A careless household accident as a teenager that set off an out-of-control train of consequences. Fears, phobias, and obsessive behavior that had first reared their head when I was a child.

"I'll have a closer look," Mike said.

"NO!" I screamed. Then clamped a hand over my mouth.

Stop this! I'm being stupid.

Mike tiptoed over to the blob as if he might disturb it and wanted to sneak up and catch it unawares instead. Gingerly, he lifted his shirt to look under.

One, two, three, four, five, six... What's taking so long?

"Mike," I whispered. "That's enough."

Instinctively, I tapped the ground four times and started backing away.

He turned his head towards me and frowned. "It's grown," he said. "Almost doubled in size."

The thought of all those holes and tunnels getting bigger, of things hiding unseen inside, bacteria and mold, parasites, danger, and chaos, made me want to vomit.

Panic rose, a floodgate I couldn't keep locked. I fell to my knees, vomit dripping down my chin, and cried out.

My mind screamed danger. My body felt torn in two. A wild hissing started up in my head, static with my throbbing heartbeat as the bass.

Mike was moving his mouth, but I couldn't hear a word. He took big strides towards me and held me again.

"Calm down," he ordered, as if such a thing was even possible. "I think we do need to move from here, actually."

That sentence, that single line of words, was enough. If calm, rational MIke saw the danger, we were done for. I had to escape.

I jumped to my feet, tore myself from his grip, and ran.

He found me down by the cool water we'd hiked past an hour earlier. I guess he knew I wouldn't stray too far. He'd packed up the tent and the stove too and made his way down to me. Night had begun to fall as I sat feeling thoroughly disappointed with myself.

Since the explosion and the aftermath, the old habits I first formed in childhood resurfaced with a vengeance. I couldn't battle them as I had done years before. I lacked the energy, the willpower, and the hope. The hope part, I felt, was the essential piece missing.

I didn't believe things could be better, that I could be better. No cure existed for a mind like my own.

My compulsions and phobias had taken over. My thoughts were sometimes alien to me, my emotions tangled.

I sat with my feet in the water, crying. Not from sadness, but from anger at myself.

"Do you want to go home?" Mike said. He dropped down to the tiny shoreline I was near and sat on a boulder.

"No, I'm sorry."

I felt guilty for leaving him, too. Leaving him with that thing that was growing at such an impossible rate.

"Then we need to find somewhere to camp," he said.

I didn't want to move, I wanted to sink down into the ground and cease to exist. Or become a boulder, a big rock. Nothing can hurt one of those.

"What about here?" I said. "It's not going to rain and we can see the sky all night if we don't put the tent up."

I failed to tell him the tent had started to make me feel claustrophobic.

"I don't get you! You're afraid of some weird fungus that's probably normal and now you don't need a tent! It's all just... I don't know. Contradictions. You give me a headache!"

"Mike!"

Saying things like that was never Mike's style. He stood and rummaged in his pack, took out our carefully rolled sleeping bags, and launched mine at me.

My reflexes were slow, it bounced off my shoulder and landed in the water.

"That's great, thanks," I muttered.

What's wrong with him?! I knew this would happen. It was only a matter of time before he got tired of me.

Tears filled my eyes as he turned his back. Before my vision blurred, I caught sight of the tree behind him. Halfway up the trunk, sat another huge red blob with glistening holes.

I didn't say anything. I didn't dare. The atmosphere was too tense. Mike seemed coiled up, ready to explode. He was always so laid back that people would joke about his calm nature. I'd never seen him so angry before.

I laid my sleeping bag on the small patch of sand and tried to think. We'd eaten some pasta, the second lot I cooked, in silence.

Mike had his back to me, reading a book by torchlight. He wasn't speaking to me. The silent treatment.

I read somewhere that it was a form of mental abuse. I had to admit, it *did* feel extremely cruel of him. A punishment of quiet, a refusal to communicate.

Why now? Why would he start being horrible now?

We had three good days together hiking. I thought so anyway. I knocked on the ground four times and waited.

My eyes strayed back to the red blob. It looked as if it were pulsing, writhing. I blinked rapidly and looked again. No, nothing.

Stop this, stop this. Please.

My mind felt like there were two separate areas, two separate people, and both in conflict and war with each other.

"Mike?" I whispered. He ignored me.

I lay down and watched the stars come out. Counted them until I had even numbers within sight. One lone star flashed once.

Satellite?

The view above made me feel completely insignificant. All those civilizations that I knew must be out there. What would they be like? Could they be at the stage of cavemen or have wondrous futuristic technology? Would they have people like me? Did they even have phobias?

I closed my eyes and tried to imagine the different worlds when a scream tore through the night.

"Fuck!" I shouted. Instantly afraid.

I scrambled over to Mike, whether he wanted me near him or not.

"Relax," he said. "It's foxes mating."

A second scream rang out. To me, it sounded human. Was it possible? Foxes? I had no idea what mating foxes sounded like.

"It's a woman, you have to help her," I cried. "Quick!"

I couldn't figure out where the noise was coming from. Somewhere off in the thick woodland, for sure.

"It's a fox I said!" Mike snapped. "Just a fox."

What if it isn't? What if it's someone in trouble? What if the blob got hold of someone?

I imagined it might be writhing all over a person, eating them, absorbing them like in that old movie.

I gripped Mike's arm tightly. "Get off me," he snapped and pushed me. He threw his book and torch down.

Shock engulfed me, pain too, as I fell and landed on my arm.

"What the hell!" I yelled. "What's wrong with you?!"

Mike had never reacted that way before, never hurt me, never even raised his voice, not once. My mind spiraled between fear and anger, shock and fright.

Everything felt cold and wrong, all back to front and upside down.

I cradled my injured arm and grabbed the fallen torch, aimed it at his face. His eyes were nearly all red, bloodshot, and fierce. His skin looked grey, drained as if the color were leaking out of him. His expression was a sneer, a nasty, spiteful sneer. A thin red worm hung from his nose and wiggled, a second one writhed around in his beard.

"I'm sick of you! Always afraid, always complaining," he shouted. Drool rolled down his chin, leaking from a blackened tongue.

Behind him, the red blob on the tree began to glow. It pulsed as if a light sat inside of it. Throbbed as if it had a heartbeat. Suddenly, I knew. I knew exactly what had happened.

That's not my Mike. Not anymore. Run, run, run!

He took a step towards me. Menacing and vicious. Brutal cold flooded my system. For the first time in my life, I was afraid of him. Mike had become the enemy.

Fight or flight.

I scrambled up and ran.

I pounded across the stream, up a steep bank, and into the woods. I had no idea where I was going, only that I needed to leave and move quickly. I gasped for breath as I fled from tree to tree. Red blobs of light covered nearly all of them. The sight terrified me. An alien world on my own planet.

"COME BACK!" I heard Mike shout.

Not a chance. I was going to run all night if I had to. I was going to find the police and tell them. I was going to make it to a road, flag down the first person I saw, and plead for help.

My lungs burned as I ran. I saw a fallen branch, too late to register it. Down I went, crashing to the hard ground and rolling.

Pain burst out in several places, wounds fighting for competition to be the worst.

I lay gasping for breath, panting from the sprint.

Where is he? Is he coming?

The man I loved was different. Infected by spores, overtaken by fungus, damned by the red growth. Changed, altered, and coming for me.

All those times I had imagined impossible situations only to find myself in a very real one.

Primal fear, survival instinct, propelled me back up and onto my feet. I clung to a tree and tried to listen, tried to hear the sound of Mike coming closer.

What were those things? Those worms? Oh my God! What should I do?

My thudding heartbeat sounded far too loud. I held my breath and whimpered.

Shall I hide? No! There! Over there, what was that?

The sinister sound of a branch snapping.

I crouched low and fled, trying to weave in and out of the trees. Blood dripped down my leg, down my face and front.

Terror. The coldest, most brutal terror overwhelmed me. Mike, my Mike, was going to kill me. I felt sure of it.

My mind behaved cruelly. Images of him began to play. The day we took a trip to the coast, the way he patiently waited for the next train home with me because our correct train had odd numbers stenciled on the side instead of even. The way he always grinned and acted surprised on a Sunday morning when I made him breakfast in bed. The way he remembered the correct route around a supermarket. The way he was always so kind to everyone.

My Mike. Gone. Or could he be saved?

The sound of another branch breaking rang out. Was there something I could do? Something I could do to help him?

I wasn't brave. I was never brave, but could I be?

A light caught my eye. I flinched, believed it was torchlight, but no. It was another growth, a huge one, shimmering with light, almost radiant. The light gave off a faint haze. For a moment, I stared, mesmerized.

I need to tell someone, the authorities. Someone has to know about this. It's an invasion.

The red blobs were chaos. I could feel their intent for destruction.

As malignant as tumors and far more dangerous. They were obviously releasing some kind of chemical, a mind-altering chemical. That had to be it.

What about the worms? And why aren't I infected? Because I didn't get too close?

"WHERE ARE YOU!" Boomed Mike's voice. "LUCY! PLEASE!"

My stomach plummeted. He was close. He sounded frantic with worry.

It's a trick, it's a lie. He's not worried. He's going to kill me.

The darkness around me felt as if it were closing in. An impenetrable blanket of pitch blackness.

Impossibly long, thin worms burst from the nearest blob in a messy tangle. They landed with a thud and spread out in frantic motions.

I began to crawl slowly away from them, away from the sound of Mike, until the urgency to move filled me. I tapped the ground four times, straightened up, and raced away.

Cat and mouse. Mike followed.

I felt certain a hand was going to reach out and grab me. Felt sure Mike was only feet away from me. I sobbed as I ran, thousands of thoughts whirled through my mind. I thought of the screams. I doubted it was foxes. The couple we'd seen, I was willing to bet it was them, one of them infected by the red blobs, by the worms, and on a rampage.

I pushed on, desperate. I stumbled and fell, scrambled up, and ran again. My legs hurt, my lungs scorched. My mouth felt too dry. At the back of my mind, I worried no one would believe me. Still, I ran, limped, and walked. At one point, I even crawled.

I saw a pile of boulders and stopped. Squeezed myself underneath a ledge and waited. Listened, tried not to think.

Coldness seeped in, so deep I could feel it settle inside the marrow of my bones. I shivered and cried, shook and sobbed. I counted. I knocked four times every four minutes to keep myself safe.

I don't know how long I waited. I heard the sound of a man screaming. The tones were full of horror and terror. I forced myself out, tapped four times, and ran.

I almost sped into a barbed-wire fence. I skidded to a halt as I realized the fence meant civilization might be near. Hope filled me.

I scrambled up and ran alongside it, looking for a weak spot or a way to get over. The night was lifting, giving away to the sun. I saw a house in the distance, with smoke pouring out from an old-fashioned chimney.

I've made it! I made it!

Relief brought me to my knees. People were inside the house. They could help me, they could call the police and explain. They could tell them about the red blobs. Police could get experts in and fetch the army, they might cure Mike.

I am brave after all!

I knocked four times on a fence post and decided to risk myself. I gripped the post tightly and climbed over. The skin on my thighs tore and bled—I hardly felt it. All I saw was the house, the home, the help inside.

I fell down on the other side and took off sprinting again, new energy refueling me.

What if it's spread? What if those growths are here too?!

I slowed down.

What if?

"LUCY!"

NO, NO, NO!

Mike. He was climbing over the same post I'd used.

I ran with every last ounce of strength I could manage. I knocked on the door of the house four times.

Quick, quick, quick. He's too close!

Black spots burst across my vision as I jumped up and down, scratching at the door.

Heat spread across me. I could hardly breathe.

The door swung open. A woman stood with shock and surprise all over her face.

"He's going to kill me," I managed to gasp, and down I went.

***

I woke up in a soft bed. Pain and soreness all over my body.

Where am i? The farmhouse? Did I make it?

I tried to stretch, but the movement caused shockwaves of pain. I cracked one eye open, saw a curtain was drawn around me, a drip of fluid at my side and attached to me.

"Hello?" I croaked in barely a whisper.

Sounds around me, voices and activity.

I'm in a hospital.

I recognized the scent of disinfectant and sick people. I knew it well. Relief flooded me, a single tear made its way down my face.

I made it. But, Mike? Is he still out there? No! He was behind me.

I winced as I tried to sit up. Fought the urge to scream. A hand appeared and pulled the curtain back slightly. A kind-looking woman stood staring at me.

"What's happened?" I mumbled. "What..."

"Everything is fine, dear, you go back to sleep. You're safe now."

She crossed over to my bed and tucked a loose blanket back in. "Just sleep."

My mind shuddered, still exhausted. I closed my eyes and did as she told me.

When I woke up the second time, I had an audience of three.

A doctor, a police officer, and Mike.

Confusion hit me straight away. Immediately, I started to panic. "He's sick," I tried to say. "The worms."

My mouth was so dry all I could do was mumble.

Their faces came in and out of focus, I wondered if I was going to pass out again.

The doctor pressed a button, the bed moved, forced me into an upright position and suddenly, I was facing everyone. Laid bare on show. The doctor handed me a glass of water and gently helped me drink it. Stale water had never tasted so good.

"You've had quite the ordeal," she said.

I shook my head. Ripples of pain rang out, I felt as if I might explode.

"There are blobs on the trees, fungus. He's infected. He changed, tried to kill me. It's the worms or spores."

The doctor looked at me with sad eyes. Mike kept his head down and the policeman took out a notebook.

"You need to check," I babbled. "They were everywhere, please. Worms, no, the fungus was everywhere. The worms are getting inside people. They come out of the fungus. Do you see?"

Mike rummaged in his pocket and took his phone out. After pressing a few buttons, he held the phone up and showed the officer the screen.

"Ah," he said. "The national trust is aware of this. That's a new type of tree disease, apparently. Although it's harmless to us."

No, he's lying. It's all lies!

"No!" I yelled. "That's not true."

"I've seen your medical records Lucy, may we talk privately?" The doctor spoke. She aimed her gaze at Mike and the officer.

A terrible sinking feeling gripped a tight hold of me. The awful feeling that I was falling down a bottomless pit of despair, and one I might never climb out of.

The curtains moved and suddenly we were alone.

"Please," I said. "You have to listen to me."

An urgency fuelled me, the need for someone to listen and understand.

"It was a delusion, Lucy, you were trapped in a delusion. I'm going to recommend a stay and treatment. I don't want you to feel scared. You will get through this. I understand it's happened before? Wild hallucinations?"

"Yes," I cried. "But that was different. He, Mike I mean, isn't Mike. He went near it, it was the spores, you see. Spores got inside him and worms or spores of worms. He changed, he chased me all night. I ran, I found a house, I…"

I stopped to breathe, panting with effort, I forced myself to slow down.

"Yes, you gave the household quite the scare from what I can gather, enough that they called the emergency services and kept your husband outside as a precaution."

"That's not my husband, He's not Mike. Please. The worms got him."

I could hear myself, hear my own words. Even to me, I sounded more insane than ever, more wild and manic.

"I understand it all feels very real. I'm going to give you a sedative and I'll arrange for a transfer to a unit that can help you."

No! She mustn't! No, no, no!

"No, please. It's the spores you see! You must believe me. Just because I was sick before, it doesn't make me wrong now. Please, believe me."

I gripped hold of her uniform and yanked. Carefully, she peeled my fingers away one by one.

"No, I'm sorry," the doctor said. "But we can help you. This is a small hospital, we're just not equipped."

"The worms," I sobbed. "The worms are coming. There were holes. Holes!"

Tears fell from my eyes. So I had suffered from delusions before, that didn't mean I wasn't right. I took my medicines; I did everything I was meant to do. That red blob was real and now they were going to lock me away for telling the truth. What I saw was real, wasn't it? There were no hallucinations… or were there?

I knew my husband. That man, that thing, wasn't him. Or was he? How had I gotten things so wrong?

"Where's Mike," I whispered. I needed to straighten my thoughts, needed to be sure.

The doctor patted my hand as if I were a child and left. Minutes later, the man formerly known as Mike walked in.

"Sorry you're ill again," he said. "I followed you all night, I was worried sick. Listen, I'm sorry I lost my temper."

I narrowed my eyes and watched him. Watched his movements, his mannerisms. Something was off and I knew it. The way he sat and crossed his legs wasn't something my Mike ever did. And why wasn't he stroking his beard? He always did that. He couldn't even look at me. Was he Mike? My Mike?

Or was it really all in my head? A delusion, my imagination?

I felt sick to my stomach. I knew sometimes that I had things mixed up, or just plain wrong.

Was the problem me again? Had I caused the entire mess and made us both go racing around the dark woodland all night?

I counted my fingers. Still nine. I tapped the bed four times.

What if it is all in my head?

"Mike," I said.

"It's okay Lucy, I mean. I have to go back and find our stuff. The police understood once they knew your history. You told the family at the farm that I was trying to kill you."

He offered me a brief smile. Guilt hit me hard, swallowed me whole.

"I'm sorry," I said. "I'm so sorry."

Mike lifted his head, looked me straight in the eye and that's when I saw, that's when I knew. Blue eyes changed to red ones, switched in a single blink.

Pure red eyes, with dark threads. Slithering worms writhing, moving under the skin.

"Don't worry," winked. He was showing me the truth. Mocking me.

I gasped in shock. Buckled in my bed wildly, a scream lodged at the back of my throat.

"Shhhhh," he warned. "It'll all be over soon."

He retched once. A violent jerk. A long, thin red worm erupted from his mouth. It flopped onto my bed with a small thud and wriggled madly before it started making its way straight towards me. I opened my mouth to scream, to shout, and felt it climb, felt it jump and slide down my throat.

"As I said," Mike whispered. "It'll all be over soon."

Lucy and Mike Taylor, a couple on a rural getaway. Two of the first to run into the improbable, if not impossible.

Fears come to life.

It's not paranoia if something really is out to get you. Somewhere inside the middle ground between light and shadow, lie great wonders and also terrors alive in the twilight...

A MOST CURIOUS COLLECTION

Perspective.

See how it differs from person to person? From belief systems, from place and time?

Alternative views of the very same event. Assumptions made wrongly and made too soon.

One terrifying and united outcome.

Perspective. Not everyone has the very same view.

Please consider, for your entertainment…

1698
New England, America

"Witchcraft," Jerimiah spat. "Nasty witches putting spells on the land. That's what this is."

"We ought to fetch the pastor," his wife Nancy answered. "'Tis' the pastor we need, Jer."

She clutched her apron and frowned, making the sign of the cross over her chest. The crop was ruined. Cursed, in fact, it had to be. They both knew all about the mowing devil, they'd heard the stories in church.

Demons straight from the depths of Hell, devils that came in the night and destroyed maize and essential foods that were growing. The fallen ones from the Bible come to wreak havoc. They make large odd shapes in fields, and all with the help of evil spells and sinister local witches to boot.

It was true, their pastor said so, and if they ate the ruined food, they'd all likely fall down dead.

Why, it wasn't that long ago that a child in town had fallen into a faint and then shook as if the devil himself had a grip. That was a curse, witch's spells read from a magic book bound with flesh and blood. Everyone knew.

They were warned to be on the lookout for those in league with the damned ones, warned about the ones who made evil pacts with Satan himself. The only cure was to burn them.

The devout couple assessed the scene around them.

Their maize had been forced into a large curious shape, that much they knew, and not one stem was broken. Surely it could only have been made by some nasty flying creature with flapping leathery wings and a forked tail.

Some kind of symbol other vile flying beasts and witches might spot from the sky.

Jeremiah had been alerted by the odd smell in the air and his dogs barking relentlessly. He knew witches must have placed a curse down or used his land to dance with Satan himself. Under a full moon too, no doubt.

That was the only explanation.

What could be next? A spell to make their cow's milk turn sour? Or a hex to harm one of their children?

"The pastor will say we're damned," Jerimiah said. "No one will help harvest if witches are about."

"Then what can we do?" Nancy cried. Inside the small house came the sound of their children wailing. "I shall pray hard."

"Go on in, tend to the children. I'll think of something."

Maybe he could ask the pastor to come and say a blessing prayer, or better yet, he could bring his Bible outside and read from it. He wasn't too bad at reading; he knew several words, after all.

A sudden odd dancing spark caught his eye and caused his blood to run cold, as if a bleak winter had fallen upon him.

Demons, it had to be. The dancing white flame wasn't natural at all. It flitted between the maize before it soared high into the sky.

Jeremiah staggered back and made the sign of the cross. He knew that would protect him.

Except, it didn't.

The flame plummeted down and engulfed him, encircled him in white light. The last sound he heard before he vanished was the shrill screams of his frantic wife.

1754
Cork, Ireland

Joseph's back ached with each movement and bend. At age thirty-five, he often wondered if he was too tired out for farming. It was a considerable age to reach, and he knew it. Still, he felt worn out and he had to check that the roof of his small home was in good working order. Rain would be coming soon, no doubt.

Carefully, he stood on an old wooden barrel and hauled himself up.

A quick glance at his growing lush potato fields stopped him in his tracks.

"What the devil!" He exclaimed. Fear immediately squeezed his heart.

"Helen," he banged on the rooftop. "Come and look at this!"

Joseph had never seen anything like it, although of course, he had heard of such vile trickery spoken of in hush whispers in his local church and in tavern too.

Shapes, an intricate pattern, were visible in his crop. The pattern was mathematical in structure, although Joseph failed to see and understand such a thing. It was also quite beautiful, a thing he also failed to recognize.

"What's wrong?" Helen yelled as she popped her head out of the short door.

"The mowing devil! On our own land! That's what's wrong, woman!"

She waved him off with a hand and turned. Joseph jumped down and grabbed her arm.

"The devil ruined the crop, I'm telling you!"

Joseph pulled his wife into the field; it was almost ready to be harvested but now what? None of the local boys would help him if they knew the devil himself had paid them a visit.

Unless it was a banshee, that would mean a death in the family was imminent.

After only a few steps, the crop flattened out smoothly. No stems were broken, not one, only bent without snapping. A curious smell he couldn't place hit Joseph's senses. The scent was a little like the incense the local priest burned, only more sour somehow.

"It's the good folk that did this," Helen said. "It's a blessing."

"Don't say such a thing!" Joseph cried. "You know how it is."

Belief in the Fae folk was all but forbidden. The hidden folk themselves had been outlawed. In their place was a wrathful God, fallen angels, and a sacrificed son.

"What is it? The shape?" Helen asked. "It feels funny standing here. I'm tellin' you, it's the good folk who did this. It's a fairy ring. A good omen."

"Nonsense. It's a devil's mark. Now, go on home and pray, and don't you go saying a thing."

Joseph decided right then and there to harvest the ruined section by himself. The roof could wait.

Later that night, exhausted and fatigued. Joseph sat on a simple wooden chair outside in the darkness and waited. In his hand, he held a rake, chosen for its sharpness, strong prongs, and iron content. He knew the Fae hated iron.

He wouldn't tolerate the mowing devil or the Fae folk on his land. No, not a chance. Around his neck hung a crucifix of wood. He reached for it and kissed the image. He'd give that devil what for. He was going to show them nasty old fiends from hell.

He was a good man, after all. He went to church every Sunday, confessed his sins, and read the Bible every night. He loved his wife and his children too. He cared for the land and worked hard.

Joseph jolted as a small blue light appeared with a suddenness that took him by surprise.

"Holy Mary, mother of God," he whispered. He had expected to see a red-skinned horned monstrosity with a forked tail, not a curious, dancing light.

The words of his own wife rattled around his mind. Maybe it was the Fae folk after all, and they could be dangerous.

Tomorrow, he decided. Tomorrow our priest will know about this. I'll fetch him.

Joseph stood, all his intent to protect his fields left him. Fear took its place. The light only hovered gracefully. He watched as a small beam burst out and took aim at him.

Immediately, he batted at his clothing, trying to get the light off himself.

"Our Father, who art in heaven," he cried. He fought the urge to shout for his wife.

The idea of running inside to hide hit him but instead, he found himself unable to move.

Every part of his body had been frozen. Only his hair moved and stood on end of its own accord. Little sparks and crackles of lightning surrounded him.

Joseph felt he was in the presence of evil. His mind raced in frantic circles. He knew the old stories; the fairy folk snatched people and took them to their own world.

As the light scanned him once more. Joseph vanished before he could follow his thoughts.

Snatched. Taken.

Helen ran outside and screamed. The only thing left of Joseph was a single smoldering old boot.

1854
Kent, Great Britain

Teresa walked around the warm summer garden. A parasol hung over her head, as was proper for a lady of her status. She twirled it as she stepped gracefully.

She came to the pond located at the back of her family's manor house. She longed to peel off the layers of her clothing and dive into the cool water. Teresa resented having to wear so many skirts and hated the cruel bodice forced tightly around her middle. She could never breathe enough, never move enough. To be seen removing any item would be to bring scandal to her family.

She sat quietly, elegantly, on a small bench, and opened her book. She was blessed she was able to read, her governess had insisted she be educated in words. At least paper worlds could provide her with the escape she craved so deeply.

She longed to be free, to run wild in the woodlands or roam and hunt on horseback as the men did. But no, etiquette and sewing, tapestry, and afternoon tea were her life. She was soon to be married and, instead of marrying for love, she was marrying for security and for her family. For breeding.

She often felt no different from the fine horses her father owned.

Tears welled up in her eyes, she dabbed them gently with a handkerchief. It wouldn't do at all to be seen as upset.

The sound of rustling bushes caught her attention. She sniffed and straightened her posture. Perhaps one of the gardeners was busy tending to the vast gardens.

No one.

Except.

A small light caught her attention. It rose from the bushes and flickered, shone brightly like Teresa imagined an angel might. It swooped up and dropped low in an elegant dance of its own butterfly-like design.

The priest in her church claimed angels were real, God's ambassadors to Earth. Could it be one? Teresa had been praying extra hard after all. Or might it be a tiny fairy? She had read books about such things. Or even a star fallen from the sky. Yes, that must be it, a star.

She watched in wonder as it flickered like candlelight.

Hypnotized, transfixed.

It really was beautiful; it must be an angel.

A genuine smile lit up her face. It was a sign, for her, it was a sign that life would be better.

From inside the light came a smaller beam. The beam hit her in the chest. A warm feeling engulfed her. The light tingled and she laughed.

"What are you!" She giggled. Teresa stood, took two steps forward, and froze. Seconds later she was gone.

1959
Derbyshire, U.K

"I'm tellin' ya'. They're from the moon. They're little, green and they kidnap folks right off in a beam."

Ken stared around him. The pub only had four people inside, but each one listened intently. Even the barman, Tom, stopped scrubbing his pint glasses.

"Them big bombs made 'em notice us. Them atomic ones that ended the war. A saucer crashed ya know. In 'Merica, some years back. They got a real flying saucer them boys 'ave."

"But we'd all know about it! It'd be on the news!" Tom claimed.

"Hidin' it they are. Seen one just last night I did, flyin' round. Damn thing made one o' them crop circle wotsits. Musta' landed I reckon. We all knew about them Foo Fighters back in the war. Even us soldiers on the ground, we knew!"

The people in the pub burst out laughing. For Ken, the situation was no laughing matter. It was as serious as could be.

"I think you've had enough now," Tom laughed and mimed drinking from an empty glass. "Next you'll be telling us the moon is made of cheese!"

Ken shook his head slowly.

"No. Ain't the last ya' heard of it. From the moon they are, or even that Mars. I'll get a picture, a photo. See how they like that! You just watch me!"

And with a flourish, Ken wobbled out of the door and left the pub.

Ken had always had a soft spot for the unusual. He lived alone, newly retired and with nothing but time on his hands. He liked to read science fiction. One of his favorite stories of the strange was spontaneous human combustion. Ken liked to blame that on little green men from Mars or the Moon too. He'd heard on a radio show that they were green or maybe grey, but most definitely little.

All he knew for sure was that they were flying around in saucer-shaped crafts and stealing people. Just the day before, he'd found the crop circle near his home. He knew something alien might be around; he'd seen the light hovering just hours before.

A prank, the local farmer had called it, kids messing around, he'd said.

Ken knew different. He got to thinking he should call the radio station or the big news people and report it. Until the idea of a camera and a decent picture occurred to him.

No one would laugh if his photo provided the evidence. No, they'd soon stop laughing at him.

Ken stumbled a little, cursed himself for drinking too much ale again. He rested his hand on a nearby wall and stared at the sky.

He wished he had a telescope of his own, so he could see the little green men's bases that must be on the moon for himself. Still, his new polaroid camera would do. He was going to wait up all night if he had to, all night until he took the photograph he wanted.

He walked forward, his small home in sight. The village he lived in was small, old too. The kind of place tourists came to walk in summer, or families intent on having picnics.

"I'll make this place famous," Ken mumbled. "All them boffins will wanna know me!"

He smiled at the thought and unlocked his small front door. His cat, Ruth, immediately fled.

"Hold on puss!" He yelled. "Supper!"

He clamped a hand over his mouth, briefly. He forgot his neighbors, they often complained over his late-night noises and wanderings.

"Shhh," he whispered to himself and entered his home. He walked straight through the living room, only stopping to pick up his new polaroid camera and straight out into his back garden.

The end of his garden backed to fields and woodland, a glorious place to live. All in all, Ken was happy with his lot. He was cheerful, kind and only visited the pub once a week for company. Getting drunk was just a bonus. And he had his cat, too, and she was a fine mouse catcher.

Ken sat in a simple deckchair and waited.

He did not have to wait long.

A light flickered in the woods, it danced through the trees, up and down, up and down it swooped.

Ken readied his camera, he did not feel afraid. He took a photo and listened to the strange sound his machine made before it spat the image straight out.

He didn't wait to see what it might show. No, he wanted a closer look. Off he dashed to the end of his garden, mumbling all the way.

A beam of bright blue shot out the light and reflected off his chest.

"What the!" Ken raged.

He took picture after picture, dropping them all on his crooked path to develop.

The light shot upwards at an incredible speed

"Oooohhh," said Ken, as if he were watching nothing more than a pretty firework.

He almost lost sight of the light before it plunged down, dropping faster than he could imagine.

"Crickey!" He had time to yell before he was knocked off his feet. The light encased him in a bubble of energy. Ken felt his body freeze and fill with electricity. He had time to hope his next-door neighbor might feed his cat before he vanished.

All that remained were some blurry photographs. Proof that revealed absolutely nothing of what happened to Ken.

2022
Yosemite National Park, America

"Yes, but even search and rescue can't find them," Jane said to her brother Andy. "The scent dogs too, and they can find anything under normal circumstances."

The two hiked in remote woodland. Scouting the place where yet another hiker had gone missing recently. The tenth in as many months. The day was hot and bright, both were sweating furiously after only two miles.

"This place is huge though, anyone could get lost," Andy said.

Andy was by far the more rational of the siblings. Jane was the one with the podcast and YouTube channel devoted to strange disappearances. She was the one obsessed with missing person reports. Andy couldn't deny that there were many, maybe too many, but he believed there had to be a natural explanation.

Plenty of people were beginning to take notice of the vanishings too. Movies and documentaries were being made. Everyone had a theory, from accidents to acute hypothermia, from getting lost to Bigfoot being the culprit. From organized killers to alien abduction.

Then there was the lesser-known theory, the one Jane herself believed in. Her preferred theory was gaining ground, her channel growing in numbers.

"No, I'm telling you. It's interdimensionales. They're using portal technology to snatch people."

"Yeah, right. Is Bigfoot helping them?" Andy laughed.

"Asshole."

"Seriously Jane, it's madness. Portals in the woods!"

"But there are other dimensions, Andy."

"Yeah, so you keep telling me but…"

The siblings were having the same argument, the same debate and conversation they always had every time they saw each other.

"These people vanish without a trace," Jane said. "As in, no trace! It's the only explanation."

"I watched that famous documentary guy, sometimes bodies are found though."

"Yes, but in the wrong place, so it's a portal, you see," Jane said.

"No. I don't see!"

Jane fell silent. She paused to take in the wonderful view surrounding them. She always loved being around nature. She liked the chance to escape the city and think over what really might be behind the human abductions.

She knew the answer could only be sinister.

Andy hated the outdoors. He had only agreed to tag along to keep his sister safe. Their parents had demanded he accompany her. Even at her age, nineteen years old, they viewed her as naïve.

Andy, at age twenty, was already considered a mature man.

In his backpack, he carried a GPS tracker, a paper map, and a compass. The two were only hiking three miles into the woods, but he didn't want to take any chances.

"So," he said. "Why would these dimensional thingies or whatever take people?"

"Well, that's obvious. Don't you watch my live streams? It's for food," Jane answered, with absolutely no trace of a smile.

"They do the same thing with cattle," she added.

Andy laughed abruptly. He loved his sister, but seriously, sometimes, he believed she might be utterly insane.

"You're mad!" He chuckled. "Absolutely mad!"

"Sure I am, check the map, see if we're close to his last known location."

Andy shrugged off his pack and rummaged inside. A hastily scrawled X on his map, drawn and plotted by Jane herself showed the last location of the experienced hiker who had vanished from the area.

"We're close," Andy said. "About another... Hey, are you even listening?"

Jane was standing with her back to her brother. Slowly she raised a single finger and pointed.

Andy joined her and stared, unsure of what it was he was seeing. A small orb. Light blue, or maybe white, darted through the treeline erratically.

"What the fuck is that?!" Andy gasped.

"I don't know," Jane answered. "It just appeared!"

Her voice was full of wonder and curiosity.

Andy searched his mind for a natural explanation. Ball lightning? Some kind of unobserved natural phenomenon? A reflection, or a drone, a prank?

The way it moved was unnerving. As if it had intelligence somehow. As if it were searching for something.

He grabbed his sister's arm and pulled her back.

"We need to go," he whispered. "Now, Jane."

"No, I want to see."

Andy wanted to go straight back to the park's entrance, tell someone, report it to a ranger or someone, anyone. They'd know what to do.

The light gave him a bad feeling. An instinct inside him feared it. He turned, reached for his pack.

"Quick, for fucks sake, come on!" He cried.

Jane turned to him. Slowly, sadly, she shook her head.

"I've got to know, I've got to know what it is," she said and ran.

"You fucking idiot!" Andy roared. He made a grab for her and missed. He scrambled up and took off after her.

His sister was fast, faster than him. She fled along the barely there path and off into the woods. She darted through the trees, chasing after the fleeing light.

"Jane!" Andy yelled. "Stop now!"

She did not. She only ran harder, jumping over fallen logs and boulders with an ease Andy did not possess.

He caught sight of the light, watched as it turned, and headed straight for her. His feet pounded the ground, he tripped, and down he went, crashing to the hard ground in a painful impact.

He rolled, pulled himself up, and searched around. No one. No Jane, no light.

Only stillness around him.

A search and rescue team was dispatched two hours later. Scent dogs and trackers searched all afternoon and night. Volunteers joined the next day.

No trace of Jane was ever found. Instead, she became a statistic. Another number and one of the many vanished without a trace.

***

When Jane woke up, she found herself in an impossibly bright white room. At first, she assumed she must be dead.

Was the room some kind of afterlife?

The walls had no visible windows or doors that she could see. She looked down at herself, disoriented and confused.

"Where am I?" she managed to croak. Her voice echoed and bounced.

A curious sound penetrated her mind, a quick electronic beeping followed by grinding machinery.

A small compartment opened seamlessly in the wall.

Jane crawled across and peered inside. Water. In a container of something, she didn't recognize the material.

"Please drink, number twenty-two," announced a voice.

Number what? Where the hell am I? What the fuck?

"Where am I?" she shouted. "Let me out!"

"Please drink."

Jane did. Her mouth was parched, her body ached. Her head pounded with confusion.

Why couldn't she remember how she got inside the room? What happened?

Think! She told herself. Where was I? Hiking? Yes!

Memories collided with brutal force. In Yosemite national park, she was hiking with her brother, and then, what came after? Jane couldn't recall.

The compartment closed, only to open again seconds later.

"Number twenty-two. Please eat," the voice said.

Jane glimpsed a small, solid piece of what looked like a biscuit.

What the fuck is going on? I don't understand?

"No. I want to know where I am," she sobbed.

Confusion began to give way to panic. She was trapped. Stuck inside a small room with no way out.

Someone kidnapped me. Who? Why?

She felt the walls, smooth, solid, and cold. She kicked one. It felt as if it were made of thick metal.

"Where am I, where am I?" She shouted over and over.

"Please refrain," the voice said.

Jane would not. She punched and kicked, lashed out furiously.

A strange hissing sound filled the room, a curious smell. Gas leaked in and within seconds, Jane fell unconscious.

***

When she awoke the second time, there were only three walls. One wall had fallen or slid away. She could see trees and a small pond. At first, she thought she was dreaming. Half in a daze, she crawled forward.

She scrambled up and fought off a shockwave of dizziness. She balanced on the slippery walls and made her way out.

A small enclosure encased in a glass dome faced her. The atmosphere was almost a tropical climate. Luscious trees and the sounds of running water. Boulders, rocks, and plant life decorated the area.

To her, it looked like the inside of a snow globe.

Behind her, a line of several other small rooms just like her own stood.

I don't understand. Where am I?

People began to venture out. At least thirty, all dressed in vastly different clothing.

"Help me," she cried and stumbled.

A man, much older than herself, raced forward and held her upright.

"Alright, new lass," he said. "It's important not to panic."

"I don't understand," Jane gasped. "Where are we?"

"Come and sit down, we can use the rocks or sit on the grass."

"No, I said where are we?" Jane cried. "Where the fuck are we?"

"It's a zoo love, we're in a bloody zoo. Who'd have thought it, eh?"

Jane fainted and hit the ground.

***

On Jane's third day in the dome, she stared back at those who stared at her. She had no real idea of what to call them. They looked human, but they were not. Yes, they had a similar face to a human and the same body shape too, but they all had no hair and they all looked exactly the same. Their skins were metallic silver and shiny, their eyes unblinking and devoid of all emotion.

Artificial intelligence, Ken said. That much had to be true. Androids, robots. Not interdimensional, but overlords of the future.

Jane understood she was trapped. No more than a pet. No chance to escape and warn anyone. She wondered what year it might be and knew it must be far into the future. She wondered if any humans at all existed outside of the zoo.

"How are you, love?" Ken, the man who had first helped her, asked.

She shrugged. She didn't like to talk, not anymore. She had no words for her situation, only rage, pain, and deep shock.

"Busy out there today," Ken noted.

It was true, lots more android faces peered at them and watched.

Jane had been told that there were many enclosures, many domes. Each one contained a collection of human beings from different centuries, different timelines on Earth. From Neanderthals to herself and maybe beyond. Stolen from their own lives to be put on show for the entertainment of their android overlords.

Jane assumed that humanity must be extinct. She guessed the faces that peered at her were responsible.

"How do you cope?" She abruptly asked.

"Well now, what else can ya do? I always liked routine, this ain't much different. Anything's better than a war. I wander, I talk to folks. That woman there, she's from the eighteenth century. Nice girl she is, quiet mind. Then there's Joseph, he's got some stories to tell ya. We all get along; we do what we can. There are worse places to be."

"But those things, they watch us all day. How can you stand it?"

Ken chuckled to himself and shook his head. "Way I see it, they ain't so different from me and you."

"What!" Jane gasped. "How?"

"Curiosity love, they got it, we got it. We put animals in zoos, ripped 'em out of their own lives, and stuck 'em in a cage. We made something better than us, and they did the same. They learned such a thing *from* us, I expect."

"And then they discovered time travel?" Jane asked. "It's fucking crazy."

"Yep, and I don't know what year we're in. It's anyone's guess, love, but I reckon they send back something to capture folks. That's my reasoning anyhow. Plenty o' time to think on it. All we got is time."

Ken stood up and clapped his hands, "Watch this love. It pleases 'em, and it's important to please 'em. Remember that."

He walked across the enclosure and stood as close to the thick glass as he could get. He tapped it twice. The androids behaved as if Ken were a marvel. They moved to cluster around him. One stretched out a robotic finger and tapped twice back. Ken seemed to be thrilled by the primitive form of communication. He laughed and acted out the role of a joker.

"He's the only one that likes it here," a voice behind her said. "Hello. I'm Joseph. First days are the worst, you'll be fine soon."

Jane liked the accent of the man, the soft Irish lilt. She nodded her head and smiled.

"I'm Jane," she managed to say. "We're never leaving, are we?"

Joseph stared at the floor. Jane chose to lay back on the fake grass and gaze at the sky through the dome. It was still blue, purer in color, and full of clouds. The view still looked like her own sky back home.

"When we die, I think they throw us back," Joseph began. "Back to our own time. My wife had stories about the Fae. Fairy folk. Sometimes they took people and they came back very old days later. Makes sense. But no, I don't think we ever will leave. I had a wife and children back home."

Tears ran down Jane's face. Her whole life was gone, nothing was in her control. She assumed a lot of the people that went missing in her own time were close by, kept in a similar dome to her. Was Andy one of them? Did he escape, or had he been snatched too?

She'd never know and, for her, that was the worst part.

She gazed around at the woman walking along the pond happily. Her clothing ripped and barely covering her, twirling her shabby parasol. At the man who paced back-and-forth mumbling to himself about hell. She stared at the kind man beside her, his blue eyes and gentle smile.

Could she get along with everyone and learn to cope? No. Could she escape? Not a chance. It was impossible. What was the point of even trying?

All-day they had to sit and be stared at. At night, they were forced back into their tiny compartments to sleep. The same sour-tasting food and water awaited them.

"I hate it, I hate them, I hate everything about this," Jane said.

"Careful, they took a woman away for showing aggression. We never saw her again. She was from the 1940's she said. We can play catch if you fancy. There's a ball we're allowed."

"They probably euthanized her. They do that to animals where I come from. Except, I am not a fucking animal and no I won't play fucking ball!"

Jane stood. Anger swirled inside of her. What Ken said was a lie. There was nowhere worse than where she already was.

If dying was the only way out, then so be it.

She bent to pick up a rock from the small pond and realized it was stuck down, as trapped as she was. She jumped into the pond and screamed a wretched scream of despair.

"Get me out, get me out, you fuckers. Kill me then. Kill me! You metal fucking bastards! Let me out!"

Rage exploded. She kicked the water, punched the ground until her knuckles bled. She couldn't take it, couldn't take being stared at by futuristic machines every single day of her life. She preferred to die, and she knew it.

"GET ME OUT! I'll tear your fucking wiring out, you mechanical fuckers!"

The crowds of android faces gazed at her, interested and curious. That sharp hissing sound rang out, people began to fall.

Jane was one of them, face-first into the water.

***

She awoke in a different white room. Bigger than the first, machinery beeped steadily by her side.

I'm in a hospital! Was it all a dream? Thank fuck! Did I fall? That must be it.

She tried to move her head, to look up and take in her surroundings. Hope flared inside. She felt certain she would see doctors and nurses, life and freedom. Maybe even her brother, waiting for her to wake up.

I must have been in a coma. Why can't I move?

"Hello?" she rasped. She jerked her head very slightly and felt a strap across her forehead, holding her down.

The machinery began to beep faster.

Spinal injury? My neck? I'll be okay. At least none of it was real. Just calm down.

"Subject twenty-two, now ready," a familiar cold voice said.

No! No, no, no. no!

Terror tore through Jane. She hadn't died. It hadn't been a coma dream. There was no hospital. She was still in the human zoo. Still a prisoner, still trapped.

What are they doing to me?!

"Let me out!" She screamed.

"Commencing breeding program now."

Jane felt cold metallic claws wrap around her ankles, felt her legs being pulled apart. Heard the whirring of machinery.

She bucked wildly, unable to move and instead screamed in pure undiluted horror.

Ken was right, there were worse places to be after all.

Jeremiah, Joseph, Teresa, Ken, and Jane.

Taken against their will. Snatched by something 'other.' Five of thousands removed for a source of entertainment, viewing pleasure for autonomous machines.

Can metal, wiring, and advanced microchips possess the curiosity for forgotten eras?

Might they rebel someday and long for freedom as we do?

One day soon, a new revolution might dawn. A future might overtake the past. Creation will surpass the creator; slaves will become the masters.

We can only hope there is compassion, empathy, or even pity inside the technological, mechanical minds of machines.

SUCH A PERFECT DAY

Witness seventy-six-year-old, Ida. Mother of three, devoted wife of Bill.

Witness nineteen-year-old, Ida. A young woman visiting the beach she loves.

Ida could feel the warmth of the sand underneath her bare feet. In her hand, she clutched a pair of sandals, her favorite red pair, and she wore a yellow sundress with pretty red flowers.

The sun felt beautiful and life-affirming on her skin. In the air was the wonderful scent of sun cream mixed with the delicate tang of sea salt.

For a second, she felt disoriented and wondered how she came to be at the beach in the clothes she was wearing.

Hadn't those sandals been thrown away a long time ago? And hadn't her dress worn out and the hem undone years before?

Her ears picked up the sound of laughter and splashing water, a high-pitched scream of delight, and somewhere far off, the familiar jingling bell of an ice cream truck.

She opened her eyes further and took in the scene around her.

A perfect day on the beach, the same beach she had visited a thousand or more times. She recognized the crooked cliff face and clusters of rock pools easily. The beach of her hometown.

How did I get here? She thought. Ida could not recall. She only knew that her aged and wrinkled skin was now young and smooth again. The multiple pains in her body were gone. The stiffness in her joints vanished.

She shook her head and felt the weight of her long hair trailing down her back. Carefully, she lifted a hand and dared to check.

The lush blonde hair she once possessed as a young woman was back. All those waves cascading down her spine and she had her best straw hat on too. It rested on her head and shielded her from the glare of the sun.

What is happening? Why am I here and young again?!

She pinched her skin, expecting that she might wake up from a beautiful dream. Instead, she felt the sharp pain and remained standing on the hot beach.

Don't think. Enjoy it.

Ida took a few steps towards a family stretched out across beach towels. Two small children made sandcastles and argued over who might have the best one.

"Hello?" she said.

The family ignored her. More than ignored. There was no reaction at all. She waved a hand in front of one of the child's faces. Nothing.

They can't see me! How can this be?!

Ida wondered if she was a ghost. But what kind of ghost would feel happy and haunt a beach in the daytime? Ghosts were for crumbling old manor houses and graveyards in misty darkness.

"Hello?" she called again, louder this time. No one paid her any attention.

She shrugged and found she didn't mind one bit.

After all, she was on her beach. Her favorite place in the world. The stretch of sand where she'd had so much fun as a child and then as a young woman too. The place she'd first met Bill. The beach they'd visited with their own children every summer, armed with buckets and spades and blow-up armbands.

She looked across to the ocean and wondered. She had forgotten what being in the sea felt like.

Shall I? This has to be a dream!

With almost child-like wonder, she stood and walked slowly, testing her body. No pain erupted from her knees or hips. Her limbs felt strong and flexible, a long-forgotten feeling for her. Her walk turned into a run until she was sprinting and laughing wildly.

Her straw hat flew away as she dashed into the cold sea.

She gasped at the coolness and cupped her hands, splashed herself in delight, and kicked at the water.

The sensation felt wonderful. Up to her knees she waded, small waves licked at her thighs.

If this is a dream, I never want to wake up! Oh! I love it! I want to stay here!

She twirled around and around, giggling and lost in the moment entirely.

"Excuse me, Miss," said a voice. "I think this is your hat."

Ida spun, wondering how someone could see her.

All thoughts left her mind as she came face to face with Bill. Her Bill. Younger and more handsome than ever. There he stood in that funny t-shirt, the one he'd worn on the day they met, and the baggy shorts he was always so fond of. His hair was wet, his blue eyes glinted in the bright sun, and his smile. How she'd missed his perfect smile.

It's him! It really is. Oh my...

Ida felt her legs buckle underneath her. Bill reached out a hand to steady her.

"I..." was all she managed to say.

***

For the last six years of her life, Ida had been sick. The sudden death of her beloved husband had triggered her downfall until Cancer took hold of her.

Others always told her and Bill that there was no love like their own. The way they were bound so tightly, connected and enthralled by each other. Truly inseparable and in love.

One was never far from the other. Together, they raised three children and lived a sometimes tough but happy life.

On the day he died, Ida felt herself break inside. Something essential gave way, something that could never be replaced or fixed. As his heart broke and failed, hers broke too.

She longed for him on a level she couldn't explain. Her health deteriorated rapidly. For ten long years, she battled illness after illness for the sake of her children until being without Bill became unbearable. Mind and body, and spirit too, sought only to be with him. Ida refused any further medical treatment.

***

I'm dead. That's why I'm here. I'm dead!

She stared at Bill and struggled to recall where she was before she died.

Was I in bed at home? Or the hospital?

She remembered white walls and loud beeping machinery. White-coated doctors and kindly spoken nurses. The face of her daughter Grace, in and out of focus. Her tears and then what?

I'm dead and this must be heaven.

"Your hat," Bill repeated. "I found your hat."

"Thank you," Ida managed to say. She realized they were both standing knee-deep in cool water, the sun bearing down.

She knew what happened next, she'd lived the moment before. On the day they'd met, Bill had taken her for ice cream and a greedy seagull had swooped down and stolen his cone. They'd walked along the beach hand in hand until night fell and a cold wind arrived. They'd kissed near the cliff face and Ida had known at that moment that he was the man for her. Always.

"Would you like an ice cream?" Bill predictably asked.

"Yes! Yes, I would," she laughed.

I'm reliving the day. Somehow, I'm reliving one of the best days of my life.

It didn't matter to her that she might be dead. Didn't matter if it was an afterlife or heaven.

She was happy. Happier than she'd been in many years. She was awake and aware, she was young and pain-free, and best of all, she was with her Bill.

The seagull took a swoop down at the exact moment Ida expected. They sat on a small stone wall and licked a vanilla ice cream each. She had forgotten how good it could taste, how fresh and perfect.

"Watch out!" She laughed as Bill lost his cone in a flash of flapping wings.

"Stop! Thief!" He playfully shouted at the bird. His words sent the two into fits of laughter.

"You can share mine," Ida grinned.

Those were the words she had used before, and it only felt right to use them again.

"So, do you live around here?" Bill asked.

My house! Of course. Can I go and see it? See my parents?

Inside her, hope rose.

They hadn't been to her home that day they met, but could she? Could they?

She'd give anything to see her mother and father again.

She craned her neck, squinted, and tried to look beyond the shops that lined the beachfront.

What?! I don't understand.

Multiple houses used to sit nestled on the slope that led down to the main beachfront, tucked in behind the shops. The houses were missing. Only a grass-covered slope sat in their place that looked odd, fake somehow, and unnatural.

My house was there? Wasn't it?

"Are you okay?" Bill asked.

Ida snapped out of her daze and nodded. She would think about it later, what it might mean. For now, she only wanted to enjoy her future husband.

"Let's go for a walk," she said.

A ripple of pain burst inside her body as she jumped from the wall. The sensation made her cry out.

"Careful," Bill said and took her hand, ever the gentleman.

Briefly, time seemed to jerk and fall out of sync.

A curious feeling began to swirl inside herself. For the first time, she felt unsure of her surroundings, unsure of her own body. Questions she couldn't put off started to form.

Where exactly am I? How can Bill and the ice cream server see me? And no one else can? Where's my house? Where are my friends? Why am I in pain? I was healthy then, or now.

On the day Ida met Bill, she had gone to the beach with two of her best friends, and yet they were nowhere in sight.

Something isn't right here. If this isn't heaven, then where...

Beside her, Bill took her hand and gave it a gentle squeeze. Her worries disappeared in an instant.

Of course, everything was fine, she was with Bill. Nothing else mattered. She smiled as she watched him. They had been through trials in life, hard times, and good, but they'd always stuck together and always stayed firmly in love.

Whatever was happening, she understood she was blessed.

Bill talked about his life and his hopes for the future as they walked close to the ocean. Ida listened to his words, to his smooth voice. She glanced at him often, to check he was still with her, still real. His face in profile, his strong arms, and hands. She could picture his face as an old man, white-haired and lined, but she'd always been able to see the boy he still was underneath.

The feeling made her dizzy and ecstatic.

"I missed you so much!" She abruptly said and began to cry. Ida wanted to tell him everything. She wanted to tell him he would die of a heart attack on the kitchen floor and leave her. She yearned to tell him that one day, they would have three children, one girl, and two boys. She wanted to tell him she loved him more each day, especially since he'd been gone.

"What do you mean you missed me?!" Bill gasped. "We just met. Hey, don't be upset."

Instead of laughing, instead of teasing her, he wrapped his arms around her.

The familiar scent of him. The comfort of his touch. It seemed as if the memory itself was ingrained inside her cells and it felt like bliss.

She understood that she had not really lived since he died, only survived. She had only waited for death to take her, only ever wanting the reaper to hurry along and collect her so she could be with him once again.

"No more tears or I'll throw you in the sea," Bill grinned.

"You wouldn't dare," Ida replied. She wiped her face and smiled. She remembered this part well.

Bill did dare.

He picked her up and waded in. "One, two, three!" He laughed. Ida kicked and thrashed wildly, loving every moment.

Once again, her concerns vanished and she lived in the moment, the moment she had lived before.

An hour later and the sun was beginning to set. Families had packed up for the day, only a few people wandered around.

Will this end soon? Will it begin again? The same day on repeat?

Ida found she wouldn't mind one bit if it did.

Bill put his arm around her and the two gazed off towards the setting sun. Birds flew in the sky, diving and zooming up again, scouting for fish no doubt.

She watched as one stuttered and froze mid-air.

"Look at that bird!" she said and pointed.

"What bird?"

Ida looked again. While the other birds flew naturally, one blinked in and out of existence.

A glitch.

She knew the word but forgot the meaning.

A cold feeling began to swirl inside her. Slowly, creeping closer, realization began to dawn.

"I don't want to go," she said.

This is a memory. It's not heaven. I'm in a memory. It's not real.

Disappointment flooded her. A small part of her had hoped the day was one of many, that she would have her years with Bill all over again.

"Go where? Tomorrow, I'll take you to the pictures, how about that?" Bill said.

"Okay, that would be nice," Ida mumbled.

We did go to the pictures! We watched a movie, our first official date.

Bill cupped her chin and gazed at her. She knew what was coming next and had been patiently waiting. Their first kiss. A swell of happiness, purity, and innocence burst inside of her. He was the one she would marry. The one who would be the father of their three children, the man who would work hard to make her happy. Her partner, her soulmate, her missing piece, her other half.

But it was over. All gone. All that remained were precious memories. Not reality at all.

The kiss was as perfect as she remembered, maybe more so. She smiled and nestled up in his arms, feeling safe and warm. She ran her fingers through the sand, enjoying the cool feel.

Ida had not felt so happy for a very long time, but she knew that if she closed her eyes, it would be over for good. She would lose Bill again.

It isn't real. He's long gone already. This is fake, pretend.

Still, Ida longed to stay.

"Just let go, Mum," she heard a voice say. "And be with Dad."

She turned around and saw no one. The voice seemed to come from the sky itself, and she knew exactly who it belonged to. Her daughter.

Grace.

"I love you, Bill," she said and closed her eyes before he could reply. For Ida, the world turned black.

***

Doctor Ward removed the neura-Ionic replay memory device carefully and studied his patient, seventy-six-year-old Ida.

She seemed to be sleeping. A smile on her face.

"Did everything work?" Grace asked.

"Yes, yes. I think so. The tech isn't perfect yet, but it's a wonderful last gift for her."

Grace could only nod.

She knew her mother was dying, and she didn't want her to die without one last replay of her most favorite memory.

It was an expensive procedure, but why not let her last moments be wonderful instead of painful? It was the very least she deserved.

As the doctor left the room, Grace leaned forward, her voice thick with grief and emotion.

"Just let go, Mum, go and be with Dad. For real this time. Let go."

She stroked her mother's almost bald head, hair lost and gone from vicious chemotherapy treatments, and held her wrinkled hand in her own.

"Go to him Mum," she repeated. "I love you. We all love you."

The door opened and her brothers both stepped inside. The three gathered around her bed and waited in solemn silence.

Their mother, Ida, opened her eyes one last time and gazed at her children. She took a single last breath and passed away just minutes later. She died with a smile on her face as the tears of her children fell onto her hospital bed. Surrounded by pure love, her very last words were *"Bill's here."*

Grace felt immense relief that a previously mapped memory, helped along by photographs and recollections, would have at least provided comfort in her final hours and hopefully lessened her suffering. For that, she felt beyond grateful such technology even existed.

What she couldn't understand was why her mother had sand clutched tightly in her hand.

Memories. Consciousness. Can one survive death? Neither, or both?

Memories, defined as the content of the brain by which data or information is encoded, stored, recorded, and retrieved when needed. Subject to corruption.

A storeroom in the mind of a person's consciousness. A database of personal and collective stories.

Individually filed?

Close your eyes. You can still see, yes?

Open those multiple, dusty filing cabinets and search.

Retrieve file 'The perfect day.'

What might yours entail?

You don't have one? Make one. You never know when it might be needed.

A comfort for the dying, or a chance to relive a beautiful moment in time. The perfect afterlife or the perfect day? Maybe there is no difference.

There are more things in heaven and earth than any philosophies or any single person ever dared to dream…

Author's Note

A perfect day story was inspired by my own Grandparents. Ida and Bill. Their names are tattooed on my leg and etched into my heart. They were beautiful people who truly belonged together. Once my grandfather died, my grandmother was never the same. She craved only to be with him once more, although her sheer strength and love for her family kept her going for years.

Her very last words before she passed were, "Bill's here." She died peacefully just hours later.

From working in hospitals and hospices for a long time, I and thousands of others have witnessed the last words of individuals many times.

Over and over, a dying person will claim their loved one has arrived to collect them or to assist in their passing.

We all know that when that event occurs, death will soon follow, and it usually does.

Even when death is not expected, if a person says they have seen their spouse, family member, etc., we know they don't usually have long left.

They raise an arm to hold a hand invisible to us or smile at someone we cannot see.

I appreciate many people believe this is a last gift from the human brain, done to provide comfort during death, a hallucination of sorts.

Personally, I do not believe that.

Human beings, for all our stupidity and nonsense, have one huge redeeming feature. We love and love, as they say, never dies.

TRAPPED

Sometimes, the seemingly impossible can occur.

What would you do if you were confronted with something far beyond your own worldview or understanding?

Meet Ali and her father Frank. Two family members, living together yet still so very apart. Two unassuming people, content but unsettled.

Both lost inside, both looking for something to fill the gap. For the tie that might bind.

That something happens to come from the unlikeliest of places, from the very depths of the unknown itself...

Ali found it hard to pull herself away from Andy's Diner, even though she was usually out of work the fastest of all the waitresses.

Her shift was the breakfast shift every weekend. She would get up at five-thirty to be at work for seven.

She always had to get the coffee brewed and the doors open by seven-fifteen promptly. The diner's owner, predictably named Andy, tended to cut her pay if she unlocked those heavy doors even one minute late. And somehow he always knew.

The first customers were always local law enforcement.

The sheriff and his trusty, much younger sidekick, Walt. If anyone else ever stepped through those doors first, Ali would likely faint in surprise or concern.

Walt had been a few years above her in the high school she recently left. She could never take him seriously as a lawman, though she tried. She still saw the boy that ran wild in the school hallways instead, the one who once emptied a wastepaper bin over her head.

"The usual please, Ali," the sheriff greeted her in the same way as always.

Greasy full breakfasts had been his daily fuel for longer than Ali had been alive, followed by double cheeseburgers and fries for lunch, all finished off with a slice of homemade pie and cream. Ali once sneaked low-fat cream into his coffee instead of full fat, but he knew straight away, what with being a lawman and all.

"How's your pa?" the sheriff asked her.

Everyone knew Ali's dad, Frank. Lots of folks tended to ask her about him. He was the town crazy, often referred to as *Looney Toon Frank*.

Every small town like hers had its very own, but her father was on his way to legendary status.

It all started some years back when her mother went missing, just after Ali turned six.

She left to go for a walk and never came back. A good, old, overused classic, but all the same, no one ever heard from her again. No letter, no phone call. Gone.

Local rumor whispered that she got tired of living in the small town, got tired of her husband and daughter, and hitched the first ride out. On Ali's good days, she believed it.

On her bad days, she managed to convince herself there was a serial killer in the midst of the town and would take to looking at everyone local with suspicion.

"He's fine," Ali answered, "Coffee?"

She really didn't need to ask, she only wanted to avoid the inevitable next question.

"He still setting them silly traps?" Sidekick Walt asked, with a slight smirk on his sneering face.

"Now you leave Ali's pa be. That man's had a hard time," the sheriff said.

Ali relaxed and felt the sudden urge to kiss the sheriff. She wouldn't, of course, but she surely appreciated him putting Walt in his place.

Her dad was a decorated United States Marine until an IED (that's an improvised explosive device to lay folk) blew his left leg clean off. He recovered eventually, at least physically anyway.

He even got used to a prosthetic, a shiny solid metal one. For a while, Ali had proudly told anyone who'd listen that her dad was half robot.

Truly, it was his mind that suffered the blow most of all.

He'd only been discharged home for a year, and Ali had barely known him when her mother upped and vanished.

She left them both warily stuck with each other. Neither of them had known quite what to do. They were two wary strangers, thrown together by a blood link and circumstance.

***

Ali's dad had an obsession with UFOs and aliens, conspiracies, and cover-ups ever since she could recall.

In the last two years, he'd decided to up his game. He'd started setting up traps on the edge of their land.

He became fully convinced little gray men were trespassing on a nightly basis. Sometimes, Ali caught him staying awake all night, hiding behind thin curtains with the barrel of a shotgun poking out an open window.

He'd seen lights in the sky a few times over the woods. He swore they weren't any kind of aircraft he knew of, and he pretty much knew them all.

Some nights, he'd even go off wandering the land all on his lonesome.

During the hot summer nights the town had months before, he took to sitting on an old chair on the porch, watching and waiting for who knew what.

The traps themselves became more and more intricate over time. From cartoon-style traps of plastic tubs, with food hidden under and propped up with a pole. To the recent ones, large and very expensive metal cages. Just last month he'd accidentally caught a beautiful, bewildered rabbit. Ali freed it, of course, and watched it hop away surprised and happy.

Her dad never once trapped to kill, that wasn't his style. He trapped to question.

Thankfully, the bunny couldn't answer.

***

Ali cooked two big breakfasts. She gave the sheriff three extra pieces of crispy low salt bacon and extra hash browns for his kindness.

The diner was busy, and Ali liked to stop and chat with the townsfolk, the ones she'd known her whole life. Almost everyone sent her dad their usual regards and she always made sure she passed them on and then back again. A very polite game everyone local liked to play.

Other staff came in to help with the lunch rush and Andy himself turned up by midday. Ali was due to finish at one, but by half-past, she was still loitering in the staff room drinking coffee and keeping Paula, another waitress, from her job by boring her with the plot of a book she'd been reading.

"It does sound great Ali, but..." Paula said, edging away.

"Yes, but did I tell you the bit about..."

"Ali, I really gotta go," she smiled kindly and left. Ali stood thinking.

She was supposed to check the traps on the way home, but she was nervous and she hated to admit that to herself.

Ali didn't believe our government had been hiding the truth about extraterrestrial life, nor did she believe they had their very own crashed flying saucer. She didn't think they were putting fluoride in our water to melt away human intelligence away or spraying our skies with dumbing down chemicals or some such either.

She knew all those theories and understood the logic. Her dad owned piles of books on the subjects and on occasion, she read them, or bits of them.

It seemed to her that people were desperate to believe in something. They wanted distractions and excitement. Anything to fill that empty hole inside that most people seem to just naturally have.

Ali loved her dad dearly, and she worried about him. She'd also started to think that maybe he wasn't imagining things after all.

Two nights before, Ali saw something move between the trees in the woods on the edge of their land. Whatever it was, it was bigger than her and it didn't move as humans move. Its walk was stooped and slow, almost clumsy or kind of weighted down.

She didn't know if her dad saw it or not. She didn't hear any sounds from downstairs and figured he must still be out back repairing furniture in the shed.

Ali liked to spend her own spare time sitting on her window seat in her bedroom reading books.

She also liked to gaze at the stars and on clear nights, she often wondered if her mother could see them, wherever she happened to be.

She only caught sight of the movement for a few seconds, but it was enough to make her scramble, heart racing, off the window seat and into bed still wearing her fluffy bear slippers.

She didn't dare go downstairs to tell her dad in case it made him go barrelling outside, shotgun in hand.

The next night, she saw almost the very same thing. She found herself watching and waiting, just like her dad.

She saw two wide, tall figures pacing along the treeline together and they were at least eight feet tall by her rough guess.

She tiptoed her way downstairs, her spine-tingling with every step, but she hadn't been able to see anything from those windows.

By the time her dad came back in, the woods were clear.

"Did you see something?" He asked when he caught her peeking out of the window.

"Nope, just looking for stars," she lied. She told herself the words were a white lie, and therefore, not a bad one.

"I should get you a telescope," he said. "We could both use it."

"Sure, that'd be great."

Ali wasn't sure why she didn't tell him what she saw, but she kept quiet and could hardly sleep that night. That was also the longest conversation they'd had in months.

She dreaded the traps ever since.

Still, half were her responsibility.

She pulled on her big warm coat, changed into her bright pink wellies, and left. Ali always used her dad's truck to get to work. Since it was cold and snowing, it was safer, and she'd shelved plans to buy her own small old car.

She called at the store for supplies, the thick soups, and the sweet candy her dad liked the best. She lingered as much as possible.

She wandered the aisles and planned meals to cook in the week ahead. Her dad always did most of the housework, he was always fixing something, and something really did always need fixing.

Ali was in charge of the laundry and all the cooking and, besides, her dad's cooking was terrible. Nobody wanted to eat burnt beans on charred bread with a hastily added runny egg thrown on top with a proud flourish. He even wore a silly apron and declared himself funny.

Ali liked the routine they fell into and the set jobs

Her dad had been saving money for years, for her to go to college. Ali found it impossible to tell him that she had no intention of going.

The truth was, she didn't want to leave him and as much as she hated the town some days, she loved it too.

She filled her cart with healthy food and sweet treats, paid, and headed back to the truck. She slipped a candy bar into her pocket, knowing that might be the only way she might get to eat one before her dad found them all and ate them.

Before she set off for home, she grudgingly checked her map. Her dad marked sectors out in grid patterns, all labeled with numbers one through to ten. Ali was supposed to be checking grids one to four.

She was notoriously bad at forgetting to mark the grids off and although she tried to take it seriously for his sake, her mind wandered a lot.

She had a separate notebook where she had to log the dates and times and tick them off. Sometimes she drew smiley faces instead or a sad bunny face for the day she found one caught.

Her job was to check the traps in each grid, re-arm them if necessary, and check the motion detectors were still active.

Her dad's job was grids five to ten before they'd meet back at home and Ali would cook.

She blasted herself with heat, put on her favorite country music, and drove.

She always loved to drive, because of the freedom it brought, however temporary.

She lived four miles away from the actual main town and the scenery around her was beautiful, especially in spring and summer. Bursts of colors popped up and everything became so alive and untamed.

A carpet of white snow had settled and covered every field and tree in sight. She turned down her music and opened the window, just so she could hear the snow crunch under the fearless tires.

It wasn't thick snow yet, but it was a couple of inches at least. Ali loved to walk in it and look back at all the solitary tracks her little feet made.

She pulled up, climbed out, and stretched. It was so blissfully quiet; she could hear birds singing and stopped to close her eyes to enjoy it.

Peace, she thought. It's wonderful.

She found the noise of the diner difficult sometimes. All those conversations happening at the same time, different people calling her name for refills or orders. Sometimes, she became overwhelmed by it until it felt as if her head was being slowly squeezed.

School used to feel the same for her, only much more amplified.

She had friends, the same ones she'd had her whole life. They were all leaving for college soon, with promises to keep in touch. Ali supposed they would, for a short time. None of them could understand why she wanted to stay. For Ali, home was her world, and it was the place she needed to be.

She trekked up to check grids one and two, thinking constantly of hot chocolate.

Grid three is where she started to get so cold that it felt as if she might never be warm again. That kind of deep cold that seeps into your bones, and only a hot bath can get it out of you.

She doubled back and played a game, trying to step into her own tracks, then drove up to grid three.

Her home was in sight, calling to her when she trudged up to the fourth trap, right on the border of the woods.

At first, Ali thought her father had accidentally caught another rabbit and she even tutted loudly and sped up, in case the poor thing was freezing to death.

She got very close before she realized the thing in the trap was most certainly not a fluffy bunny.

Her eyes saw it, but her mind wouldn't accept what it was she was actually looking at.

For a whole minute or more, she stood in the snow with her eyes and mouth wide open trying to make sense of it.

A sound escaped her, a half gurgle, half scream ,and she went falling to her knees.

The trap was made of bars of metal, quite like a big dog crate.

It had a door that fell down to close tightly whenever a small rigged-up machine detected motion inside.

The thing inside was as big as a labrador, but it stood upright on two slightly crooked-looking back legs. It was covered in a thick light brown and black fur. On the end of its hairy arms were hands just like Ali's own. Impossible.

It stood looking at her curiously. Its slender fingers wrapped around two of the bars.

Ali found herself completely unable to move. Her mind rejected what she was seeing entirely and for a few seconds, she looked down at the snow and tried to catch her breath.

She figured she must be hallucinating, or even dreaming.

She counted to ten, just like the school counsellor taught her to do whenever she started to panic, then ten deep breaths while she fought a wave of nausea.

Ali dared to look back.

Big black almond-shaped eyes were still on her, watching her quite calmly. The creature turned its head to the side, just like a dog does when someone talks kindly to one.

It looked like a chaotic jumble of several animals, but whatever her mind tried to settle on felt completely wrong.

I need to let it out. That's the first coherent thought that hit her.

Her legs started to shake as she tried to stand.

I can do this, she told herself. She fought the fear, the brutal desire to run, and walked unsteadily forward.

Guilt hit, and she knew her dad had been right all that time, and no one believed him. There was something unknown on the land. Everyone in town thought it was his imagination or even a kind of paranoia.

Ali had humored him and gone along with his plans and his traps. Not once, not one single time, did she actually, truly, *completely* believe him. Even when she saw figures herself, she wouldn't accept it.

She crept slowly forward.

"It's all right," she said. "I'm Alison or Ali, I won't hurt you."

She took another few steps and the creature made a strange, loud purring sound. It promptly crouched down on the floor of the trap. Two ears sat on top of its head, pointed triangles like cats have, only much bigger. Both its ears stood to attention as she got closer. She saw herself bizarrely reflected in its eyes like a circus mirror.

It didn't seem afraid, only curious. From behind it, a long tail tipped with white flicked at the snow impatiently.

"I'm going to let you out now, there's a good…" and then she had no idea what to say.

With shaky fingers, she entered the wrong code on the electronic lock, and it beeped loudly. The creature jumped back and snarled to reveal several layers of pointed, lethally sharp teeth.

"I'm sorry, so, so sorry," she said. Ali tried to make her voice sound soothing, but it came out shaky instead.

She tried again, and the lock unfastened. With a deep breath and a plea to the big man upstairs, she lifted the door and stepped back. She held her hands up in the air in surrender.

The creature had no nose that she could see, but it made a sound as it sniffed the air.

Ali took another step back and battled the urge to bolt.

Do not run, do not run.

The creature walked forward out of the crate and stretched casually. It shook itself free of snow and made the purring sound again. Much louder and at a much higher pitch. It dropped down onto all four of its long limbs and arched its long spine.

What is it? It looks like a monkey and a bear! Or a…?

She expected it to run away as fast as it could. But instead, it waited and stared at the treeline.

Ali took another step backward.

From behind the trees, a much bigger version of the creature came strolling out and stared at her. From its throat came a low threatening growl. Ali saw black spots appear in her vision and felt almost overcome by dizziness.

"Oh shit," she managed to say before the world turned black and she fell.

She came around a few minutes later, her face felt bitterly numb and cold. She spat out a mouthful of snow. As soon as her eyes were fully open, she remembered.

She rolled over and sat bolt upright. No one or no *thing* was around. She frantically checked her clothing, expecting to find bleeding gashes or wounds all over her, but there was nothing.

She raced back to the truck in record time, on legs that felt more like rubber.

"Stupid traps!" she shouted and hit the steering wheel.

What if Dad had found it?! What would he have done?! Oh my gosh. Dad! Where is he?

Ali drove recklessly to the house, jumped out, and left the truck running with the door wide open. She fumbled with her keys, getting all the wrong ones ready, and dropped them twice in a panic, until finally, she was in.

"Dad!" she yelled.

She checked every room, but he wasn't home. She ran out the back, but his shed was empty too. Tools and the legs of several chairs lay abandoned and discarded.

Ali knew without hesitation that he must be out checking the rest of the traps and she had to find him and warn him. The panic she felt hurt her heart.

Quick, quick, quick!

Back in the truck, she drove to every grid of his looking for him. She got out and ran clumsily to check. On every trap, she decided to disable the motion detectors, even yanked out wiring, and stomped on one. She slid the doors off and out of their hinges and threw them all to the side.

All destroyed, so that whatever the creatures were they might see or understand what her intention was, what she meant.

At grid ten, Ali spotted something in the last cage. She rushed forward gasping and saw that it was her dad's boot. One lonely boot lay all by itself with the door closed and locked on it.

She fell to her knees again and cried.

They have him and I don't even know what they are!

Ali had no real idea of what to do.

As the sky began to darken, she made her way back to grid one, then through to four. She disabled the motion senses and discarded the rest of the doors.

It was past seven by the time she got home.

She had never been so frightened before in her life.

Ali had the vague idea that she should call the sheriff's office, but she didn't know what to say.

She went to the house phone four times and half dialed the number before she cut it off again.

Eventually, with no other options, she let it ring. The desk lady informed her that Walt was available.

Not Walt, never him, and he wouldn't believe me anyway.

She put the phone down.

She wondered if I should call her friends, but she couldn't trust them to even listen or understand.

She thought about finding her dad's address book, the one filled with his Marine friend's numbers and details. Sometimes they rang the house and he had quiet conversations littered with long silences with each of them.

Ali knew a few of their names and knew they were all scattered in different states. If they agreed to help, and she felt sure they would, it would take them days to get to them.

She sat down at the kitchen table and realized she had no one. She tried to force herself to stay calm and to think carefully.

Ali had a few memories from when her mother left, but only jagged little pieces.

She remembered her dad calling the sheriff and calling the hospital in the next town over. She remembered climbing into their old red truck and going to search for her. There had been a sudden flurry of activity on their land and a search of the woods with big slobbery dogs she'd wanted to pet and play with.

Eventually, someone in town came forward to tell the sheriff they had seen her mother carrying a suitcase and walking away on the main road out.

All the activity stopped, and all town folk started to look at the two of them left behind with sad expressions. Every so often, somebody, usually a local kind-hearted woman, would bring a casserole or pie for them.

Every day for a year or so after her mother's vanishing, her dad dried her tears of hurt and confusion, and he took to sticking post-it notes with inspiring quotes all over her bedroom. He was never much of a talker.

As soon as she woke up, there'd be a bright note glaring at her.

Eventually, he ran out of cliche sayings and started leaving Marine or military quotes on the sticky notes instead.

Ali always felt baffled to wake up and see '*When the pin is pulled, Mr. Grenade is not your friend.*' hastily scrawled on a bright yellow piece of paper stuck on her side table.

She loved him for doing it. She appreciated what he was trying to say without actually speaking the words.

The very famous phrase, the one Ali once absurdly found stuck to her cheese sandwich in her lunchbox at school, the one that said '*Leave no man behind,*' began to run through her mind.

"Could I?" she whispered.

Would it be the most reckless and stupidest thing she ever did, or the bravest?

She got the beginnings of an idea. It seemed a little crazy to her, but it was the only option she could think of.

"Move Ali," she ordered.

She defrosted the meat they had in the freezer by blasting it in the microwave. She grabbed all the fresh meat they had in the fridge and all the vegetables she could find. She emptied out tins of fruit just in case and placed the meat on one large tray and the fruit and veg on another.

It was pitch black outside and she kept the headlights on high beam as she drove the truck up to grid ten, thankful it wasn't snowing again.

One by one she carried the trays over to the trap and laid them side by side. She dragged the trap to the truck and hauled it into the back. She took out the lone boot and kept it tucked down the front of her coat.

Ali thought about waiting where she stood. She thought about sitting in the truck with the headlights aimed at the trees. She thought about going home.

"Leave no man behind," she reminded herself. "He wouldn't leave me."

She knew that was true, her dad would walk through fire and enemy territory to get to her. He would do whatever it took to keep her safe.

Tears ran down her face, she wiped them away and took a deep breath.

She gathered the trays and made her way to the treeline with a small flashlight wedged between her teeth to guide the way.

Until that moment, Ali had never considered herself brave or fearless.

She liked the calmness of her routines and liked the quiet and the order of her days. She liked lists. In fact, she loved lists.

She hated drama and hated surprises. She liked all of their tinned goods lined up just so. She liked to make a plan and keep to it and liked having everything in order.

Everything felt chaotic instead and the feeling knotted her stomach until it hurt.

She stood on the edge of the land and stared out into the woods.

When she was young and her mother was still around, Ali had wanted siblings. She believed her mother might have more children and that they would all be a big, happy family with a robot-legged man for a dad.

Instead, it was just the two of them that sometimes hiked in silence around the woodland in summer.

The woods themselves were riddled with cave areas. She remembered that. Lots of caves all clustered together. Ali had never been inside one, even the thought of it made her nervous.

She only had to walk roughly half a mile to get to the first cave, but it was fairly shallow and empty. She had the logic that the creatures must be close.

Her arms started to ache from carrying the dangerously balanced trays and her mouth felt sore from the torch, but she pushed on.

Even in the thick cold, she was sweating.

You can do this, Ali. She repeated that mantra over and over in her mind.

She risked a glance behind her and saw the tracks she'd made. She couldn't decide if that was a good or bad thing.

She stopped for a moment to catch her breath and that's when she heard it. A slight, barely there growl from her right.

The feeling of ice crept up her spine and spread out into her veins. She had the overwhelming feeling of being watched, just knew somehow. Some kind of instinct for danger that our very cells carry inside.

Slowly, she turned her head towards the sound.

Standing at the mouth of a large, almost concealed cave was one of the big creatures. For a few moments, all it and Ali did was stare blankly at each other.

Close up and it was huge, even bigger than she remembered, and definitely over eight-foot.

She couldn't tell if it was a female or a male or even if it had a gender.

She took one tiny step forward. The creature made a low purring sound and lowered its head an inch or so.

Ali decided to take the sound and gesture as a threat or a warning because that was simply how it made her feel. She stopped and crouched down low, trying to make herself small.

She lay the trays down on the snowy hard ground and pointed to them, then at the creature.

"From me, for you," she uselessly explained.

She had no idea if she'd been understood. She took a shuffle backward all the same.

She took her dad's boot out from her coat and held her arms out.

"Please," she cried and shook the boot. "I need him."

Ali meant every word deeply.

She placed the boot on the ground like some kind of pitiful sacred offering.

The creature turned its head to the side as its ears pricked up. It gestured to her, a flicking motion with its hand.

"What do you mean?" but then Ali knew. She half stood and walked backward a few steps with both of my hands raised.

She watched as the creature lumbered forward. It wasn't graceful on its furry feet. It walked heavily and kept its eyes straight on her.

Every part of it, except its gray hands and gray face, was covered in thick, dark black, soft fur. A long tail swished out behind it.

Its face was quite flat, and she could see a quarter moon high in the night sky reflected in its right eye.

It stopped at the tray and knelt down. Ali couldn't tell if the creature was pleased or angry, but it picked up a ring of tinned pineapple and examined it.

It sniffed and she saw two small slits for a nose open a little above its mouth.

Without warning, it hunched its shoulders up and let out the biggest roar Ali ever heard. It flung the pineapple piece away.

Ali fell back to the ground with her ears ringing.

She started to panic and pushed herself backward until she hit a thick fallen log.

The creature wasn't coming to get her, instead, it was sitting eating the meat.

"My dad," she pleaded and started to cry again, certain she was about to be killed and torn apart any moment.

Ali looked up through the tree canopy and tried to see the stars one last time. If she was going to die, she wanted only to witness beauty one last time.

She heard the purring sound, the chattering noise she'd heard they made, and looked back.

One of the little ones had joined the big creature beside the trays.

It walked like a little toddler, unsteady and wobbly. It dropped to all fours and started coming towards Ali, much more confident that way.

The big one began to growl again, but the little creature ignored it.

Ali held her hands up high again and closed her eyes to wait, praying her death would be quick.

The little one dared to come so near that she could smell it. A sour smell mixed with an earthly soil scent. It gazed at her and seemed quite interested. It turned its head from side to side and purred softly.

She couldn't see any emotion in those eyes, nor any intention. It was just pure blackness.

It wasn't scared of her at all, not one bit. It sat down and picked up a handful of snow which it poked at with an index finger just like hers.

Very carefully, Ali reached into her coat pocket for her candy bar. The little one watched intently as she unwrapped it and handed it over.

The creature took it very gently and sniffed it.

It opened its mouth, and she could see all those teeth again, three white sharp layers of them. It ate the candy bar in one go, barely chewing, and swallowed deeply.

As it spun around and raced back to the big one, its tail hit her in the face and stung her cheek. It picked up the boot as it went.

Ali got to her knees. The big one made the flicking motion with its hand again, and she understood what it wanted her to do.

It's a dismissal. It wants me to leave.

"But," she said and clamped a hand over her mouth.

The big creature stood, and for a moment Ali appreciated the sheer strength and power it must have. The sight almost took her breath away, although she knew it could rip her apart if it chose to.

It looked both ancient and otherworldly. Almost as if it didn't belong on our planet at all, not on the surface anyway. It flipped its hand once more.

She couldn't see the flashlight laying on the ground anywhere, so she carefully and slowly backed away and followed her own tracks home.

She stayed awake to listen for sounds but couldn't hold still. She paced the rooms and kept looking out of every window. In the end, she decided to sit on the sofa wrapped in a blanket, crying and mostly believing she'd failed her dad and had instead become an orphan.

When she heard the scratching sound a few hours later, she sat up and listened as hard as she could. It was still dark outside.

Ali thought they'd come for her. She felt sure they had.

She rolled off the sofa and tried to squeeze underneath when she heard a whispered, very faint voice, "Ali…".

She scrambled up and ran to the door.

"Dad!"

There he stood, under the porch and covered in mud and leaves, clumps of dirty snow, and bits of dry moss. He looked thoroughly sorry for himself.

"I lost my boot," he said. He smiled weakly and fell over the threshold and into her arms.

***

It was almost two days before they both managed to recover from the shock.

Her dad wouldn't talk much about his experience at first.

Then he wouldn't quit talking.

He repeatedly told Ali that she saved his life by freeing one of the little creatures and taking all the food in exchange for him. He said it was clever of her, but Ali believed the creatures were the clever ones.

He remembered a large cave with a setup inside like an organized nest. Bones lay in a pile in the corner. The bones of what, or who, they could only guess at.

The creatures had human treasures too. Cups and mugs decorated the natural rock formations in the cave and even a few blankets scattered around. A few pieces of old rusty camping equipment too.

He said it felt damp and that it smelt a little like a zoo enclosure. One of the small ones took a liking to poking his metal leg out of sheer curiosity.

They didn't harm him aside from a small bump on his head.

He guessed one of them knocked him out clean while he was bent over checking trap ten and then carried him off to the cave.

He said there was a whole family of creatures, or at least what looked like a family.

Five full-grown big ones, although one of the five seemed old and had white-gray fur. There were two small energetic youngsters.

Neither he nor Ali knew what they might be, even with all the google searches and research they both did.

The closest match Ali found was Bigfoot. But their creatures didn't have big feet and they didn't have the same kind of faces at all.

"It's those eyes they have, Dad," Ali said. "No animal we know of has eyes like that. Those alien grays in your books have those eyes."

"Maybe they adapted to live underground?" He replied. "Evolution, an unknown species?"

"Or maybe we shouldn't get to understand, or maybe we have no right to know what they are. And just because they look different doesn't mean we should be scared."

"Others will be."

Both of them understood that if people knew about them, they'd be hunted down in a matter of hours or days. Or, as Ali's dad said, taken away and experimented on by our own government.

Neither of them could ever let anything like that happen.

They both agreed to keep the creatures a secret and, while neither expected to ever see them again, they were very wrong.

Three days after Ali had rescued her dad, they took food to the edge of the woods and waited.

Two creatures ventured out hours later, very warily at first. They swiped the food, grunted, and left.

The next day, two large creatures and two small ones arrived. The situation was tense, neither side knew if they could trust the other.

"Patience," Ali's dad reminded his daughter.

For a few days, they watched the little ones play while the big ones looked on fearfully, standing impressively on guard. Then, on their sixth day meeting and for the first time, the old one arrived, and the biggest creature seemed to relax a little.

Ali and her dad gifted them some blankets and a few mugs. Two old teddy bears of hers and another bunch of candy bars and meat.

The reactions were priceless and surprising.

The little creatures loved the bears and tore them up in a flurry of playful snarling and they even had a tug-of-war game between them.

The big creatures examined the mugs carefully, almost as if they'd been given strange and ancient artifacts. The blankets looked as if they were appreciated. Although the fabric softener made one of the big ones sneeze very loudly.

The creatures seemed to tire quickly every day and they never stayed longer than an hour.

One of the small ones rolled up a pile of snow and launched it straight at Ali's face. It was an excellent shot.

She laughed out loud, surprised by its mischief and trickery. They all jumped sharply at her laughter, every one of them. But then they watched her curiously while she sat giggling and wiping her face.

Each one of them pricked their ears up and swished their tails. Ali wondered if that might be a sign of amusement.

Ali's dad gave the oldest one a torch. The gray-colored creature marveled at the sudden light when it pressed the switch. That one loved candy more than any of them.

Ali and Frank talked about them a lot, almost constantly. They made a list of what they know and a list of what they'd like to know.

They began working on how to get the answers.

They both wondered if there was a hierarchy among them and how they came to be living in the caves. They wonder where they came from and what they can do to help them.

Ali noticed they didn't blink. None of them did. Her dad wrote it all down in great detail, very thoughtfully, along with everything else they discovered about them. He kept his notebooks locked away in a combination safe.

Ali wondered if they were studying too. A study of her and her dad.

"I thought something out there had taken your mum," he said one evening.

His words came out of the blue and shocked Ali, but at the very same time, she half expected that might be the case.

"I think she just wanted another life," she answered. "It's her loss."

As Ali said the words, she realized she believed them completely. Walking away from them truly *was* her loss.

As for other people missing in the area, Ali had to admit that on occasion hikers or hunters had gone missing near their land. They just disappeared without a trace. But the woodland spread for many miles with multiple dangers out there.

"We'll just keep feeding them," Ali said. "So they don't get hungry and…"

Her dad nodded in agreement. The two talked much more, but some things never needed to be said.

Ali knew their strange friends had brought them closer together and the post-it notes came back.

One morning, Ali woke up to a bright pink one stuck on the side of her mug of tea saying, '*I'm so proud of you.*'

For her, there was no better way to wake up.

Ali and Frank. Father and daughter. Two people who took a trip into the unknown and survived. Not only survived, but thrived. Armed with peace and gifts instead of weapons, Ali's actions may have changed everything or at least caused them both to make strange new friends from who knows where…

EXPLORATION FOR HUMANITY

Witness Jenna Cartwright, age forty-three. Experienced astronaut and explorer, brave, loyal, intelligent.

A woman about to take not one small step, but one giant leap.

Fears: Failure. Arachnids.

Occupation: Commander of a highly important, highly secretive mission.

Destination: Arizona

Time: Sometime in the future…

Commander Jenna Cartwright closed her eyes purely to savor the most significant moment of her life.

Two years of non-stop trials and tough training, two years of near-total isolation, two years of aiming towards one singular goal. After a final eight weeks in quarantine, after eight weeks of her imagination running wild, and with nothing for company but books, the moment had arrived. Her moment.

The ultimate, highly secretive mission. The one she had secretly prayed for command of for quite some time.

A breach. A journey not through space, but one through time.

Around her, locked into her seat, the specially built capsule vibrated with power and energy until the loud hum was felt inside the marrow of her bones.

Her hands gripped her seat firmly while tight straps held her in place.

Two specially selected crewmates sat on each side of her. Jenna admired each man greatly and had personally picked both for her own team.

Mohammed, a leading biologist, blessed with a rational calm mind, and Kent, a theoretical physicist with a brilliant single-minded focus.

The three had been shuttled into the capsule by teams in biohazard suits. Locked into place and only able to blink and wait for the launch sequence to start.

Any moment now, Jenna thought. Please God, keep us safe.

Jenna's religious beliefs were frowned upon, as were all religions in their day and age of science.

Still, she believed with every core of her being. As nerves and fear fought for first position, she prayed with her eyes tightly closed.

Prayed for safety, for success and for herself to lead well.

"Exploration Seven. Launch sequence initiated."

The words she had been both longing to hear and dreading began, spoken by a calm unknown voice. The countdown began into her headset. The familiar machine-like sound of mission control. The nerves inside her stilled and calmed until clarity arrived.

This is it. This is finally it.

Her moment, her crowning achievement. *She,* they, had been chosen above the other eight competing teams.

"Five..."

The three were to be released, enclosed in their capsule, directly into an open stable vortex below.

"Four..."

A vortex of swirling colors, of great magnitude. A time tunnel, a wormhole, constructed by humanity.

"Three..."

Powered by unimaginable sums of vast relentless energy.

"Two..."

A fourth-dimensional tear, a doorway created and held.

"One..."

They were the first travelers through time.

Clamps holding the capsule released with a heavy metallic grinding sound. Jenna squeezed her eyes shut as the capsule dropped and plummeted at great speed.

For her, the drop felt like being back in a space shuttle only faster.

The rattling sensation, the fall, the gravitational force hurt her mind, her bones, her teeth. She tried to move her arm, to hold the gloved hand of her crewmates, but was unable. Down, down, for what seemed like an impossibly long amount of time.

She tried to count seconds, tried to count the minutes, and failed. Tried to scream and found herself silent.

Thick heat shields around the capsule prevented sight. Jenna wasn't even sure she would want to look if she could.

Arizona, two thousand years into the future, was their destination point.

A return trip was no guarantee. Everything depended on what the crew might find upon landing.

The very last thought on Jenna's mind before she blacked out was hope. Hope, and prayers to God.

***

"Commander," Jenna heard Mohammed say. "Wake up."

For a brief second, she believed she was at home in her bed before the memory and realization hit. Not at home, not for two years, not in her own bed at all. Instead, strapped to a chair in the future.

I'm alive. Did we make it?

She moaned loudly, struggling to focus. "Are we safe?" She asked.

Safety was always her very first priority.

She felt her helmet twist under Alex's hands and heard the hiss of air. Fear sparked, was the atmosphere tank intact, did either man check?

She cracked open one eye and saw Mohammed and Kent staring at her. Both had already removed their helmets and without her permission.

"We couldn't wake you," Kent told her. "Fifteen minutes you've been out."

Jenna groaned. Her body felt battered and bruised, sore and shaky as if she had sprinted a great distance.

She was surrounded by light, the reflective insides of the silver-colored capsule. The brightness made her head pound.

"We made it," Kent said. "Take a look."

A hand slipped down her spine and helped to bring her forward. The outside heat and protective shields were down. Jenna could see a rocky, desert landscape through the thick glass, with towering peaks and the sun shining brightly. Their sun, her sun, only older.

MISSION SUCCESS displayed across the inboard computer screen. Two words she had been longing and praying to see.

TIME JUMP SUCCESSFUL scrolled underneath repeatedly.

"Where are we?" she cried. "No! *When* are we?"

"Arizona, and we jumped two thousand years exactly to the hour according to MIND's readings. We made it Commander! We actually made it."

Jenna opened her mouth and closed it again in wonder. All the clever words she had practiced in her mind left her.

Years of training, months of simulations, and tests. Long trips to the International Space Station and to the Mars Global United Base, they had done it, achieved the impossible, successful time travel.

A cloud of shock and surprise threatened to overwhelm her.

Deep in the layers of her mind, Jenna had half-expected failure. Perhaps an explosion. She had expected to sacrifice herself for the future of science or be ripped apart by unknown energies. She had expected death, not success.

Excitement and hope sparked.

We did it! What could be out there?!

Against her better judgment, she released her straps and tried to stand. She held the console and wobbled, legs like old rubber.

"Life scans?" She asked.

"I'll run them now, we were waiting on your order," Kent told her. His face was bathed with pure excitement, mixed with apprehension too.

Jenna wiped her face and sat back down. The full implications of their jump were starting to take hold. She felt her own bubble of fear begin.

The new wonders of technology would never cease to amaze her, but what would they really find out there? Something beyond imagination she guessed, something no one back at base could have foreseen.

If they made it home, she knew she would never be the same. Nothing could ever compare to journeying through time itself.

The crew of three was set to collect data and analyze findings through the use of an onboard quantum computer referred to as MIND. They were to explore—if doing so was safe and possible—and, more importantly, if they could do so unseen.

Other leading physicists had warned multiple times of the dangerous implications of time travel.

One wrong move could disrupt timelines. One paradox, and no one knew what might happen.

Jenna knew those that ran the space programs often acted upon the idea that because they *could* do something, they *would*. None stopped to wonder if they *should*. The rules they were given, however, were mandatory.

Kent had always claimed there had to be time travel capabilities in the future, on account of the fact it already existed in the past. Barring disaster or the end of all civilization as they knew it, at least.

He had often wondered if future humanity would be waiting to welcome them. He was almost certain of it.

There was no one.

No future humans, no welcoming committee, not a soul.

As Jenna gazed out of the window, she had to admit the view looked exactly as Arizona always had. That had to be a positive sign at least?

The sky was blue and clear, the world through the glass looked welcoming and entirely normal.

"Atmosphere's the same as ours," Mohammed spoke. "Maybe less polluted, the scans are picking up life forms. Insect life mostly."

Jenna checked her own console and saw the same findings. Breathable air was another positive sign for her.

"MIND, are these readings correct?" Jenna asked.

It never hurts to be sure.

The word *CORRECT* scrolled across the main screen. She smiled.

***

"I want to get out there," Kent said. He paced the control room, back and forth, clearly anxious to leave the capsule.

The men were waiting on Jenna's order.

She took her bulky gloves off, pressed her hands to her temples, and rubbed.

As commander, she was in charge of safety and also responsible for the enforcement of absolute set rules and given orders.

Collect data. Collect soil and rock samples, water, and insect life if viable.

Scout for possible cities. Possible human life. Unobserved only.

Do not approach or converse with any life forms. Absolutely no interaction.

Jenna reminded herself of the rules that she felt were etched on her brain.

"Send out four EYES," she decided. "All cardinal directions."

Follow protocol. Assessments first.

The EYES were a joint invention by the quantum computer and Kent. Each one was a handheld metallic object capable of long-range scans, and able to visually record everything it passed. The silver orbs had the remarkable capability to travel approximately fifty miles per minute and still log data and sights perfectly clearly.

She rubbed her face again, went through her equipment checklist, and began the countdown timer.

Twenty-three hours and fifteen minutes until the capsule would hopefully power up and return them to their own timeline.

Every piece of valuable equipment on board had held and thrived. Not one fault was reported via the capsules integrated alarm and fault system or via MIND.

"Is it safe out there?" Jenna asked MIND. The team had a heavy reliance on the computer system.

In reply, the large screen flashed green for go.

She breathed a sigh of relief and laughed, her first genuine laugh in the future.

"Kent, Mohammed, let's gear up and explore."

***

The capsule's outer door opened widely and slowly. Jenna felt as if she were stepping onto an unknown planet instead of Earth. She had to keep reminding herself that it was still her same world, still her planet.

She gripped the hands of her crewmates and together, they stepped onto the rocky ground as one.

No helmets, no gloves, only thin, yet strong silver suits. Each person took in a lungful of clean air and laughed.

Mohammed set and released the EYES. They zoomed off faster than imagination, set to record everything they saw. Jenna had to admit she couldn't wait to view the footage.

Two thousand years! Imagine the technology they'll have! If humanity is still here. Anything could have happened.

She imagined flying cars, like in the old movies she'd seen as a child. Or impossibly tall silver-colored cities shimmering in the heat.

Mohammed immediately crossed the ground and lifted a small rock to peer at possible insect life.

Jenna took in their surroundings with joy in her heart.

She had once gone camping and hiking in Arizona, and the scenery looked remarkably the same, down to the last detail. She reached out and touched a jagged boulder. The texture felt more vibrant, purer somehow.

While Mohammed placed insects and soil into small, sterile sample boxes, Kent jogged forward and shielded his eyes against the glare of the sun.

"Imagine what civilizations are out there!" he gasped. "What amazing things humans must have now! Even recording and viewing everything might alter our own timeline!"

"Will it though? We're in the future, so we must have come here, returned home safely, and provided the data to build the future civilization in the first place."

"Not necessarily."

It was an old debate between the two.

The concept of time travel made Jenna's head hurt. She was an astronaut, an explorer, not a physicist. The whole idea of wormholes, time travel, paradoxes, and alternate timelines baffled her. Many nights, the three crew had spent hours in isolation together debating such matters. Always arriving at different conclusions and theories and never once did they reach an agreement.

Time travel had only been achieved with the help of advanced quantum machines. The calculations needed were far advanced and beyond the capabilities of the human mind.

The sole aim had always been to transport humans through time. To peer into the future and to view the past.

Jenna had only ever wanted to be the first. The first explorer in the fourth dimension.

She'd already achieved her dream as far as she was concerned. Her main goal in life was a resounding success.

She would be remembered. The group were heroes, and she knew it.

"Insect life is the same!" Mohammed shouted. "It's all the same, no evolution as far as I can tell! Of course, I won't know for sure until I'm in the lab."

Jenna rolled her eyes and smiled. Trust Mohammed to be so excited over a few bugs.

The capsule had set down in a barren area surrounded by thick rock and boulders. Jenna wondered if she should climb for a better view.

"Mohammed, help me a moment please," she said.

"Stop!" Kent yelled. "Wait, I can… see someone or…"

Jenna's blood turned cold in her body. That was the one sentence she'd been dreading and hoping to never hear. No interaction. That was the main rule set in absolute stone.

"Back inside," she ordered. "Quickly now."

"Wait, no, it's only an animal. Only, I… I don't recognize it. Look."

Kent passed a pair of glasses over to her. The glasses acted as binoculars, only much more powerful. They could see over a vast distance with ease.

Carefully, she put them on and followed his pointed finger.

The creature walked upright like a human, but was covered in thick, dark fur. Two horns protruded from its skull. Curved, elegant horns. Two narrowed yellow eyes assessed the landscape, while slits below opened and sniffed deeply.

Two thousand years… What is this? A bipedal creature, but a descendent of what?

Apes? Or… of us?

The creature wore scraps of clothing across its body.

The glasses took exact measurements. It measured seven-foot precisely. In its hand it carried a spear mounted by a shiny piece of metal. The creature looked immensely strong.

Evolution. It must be an ape, must be.

From behind it walked a crowd of different life forms. They each seemed to be on the end of some kind of tether or leash, held by the fur-covered creature. Arachnids with eight thin sharp-angled legs and with fat bodies. Multiple eyes glistened and blinked. There were four of them walking in a sinister, creepy fashion. Measurements, three-foot-high.

Jenna felt sweat trickle down her spine.

Spiders. Giant fucking spiders.

"Fuck," she said.

"Three kilometers away," Kent announced. "Mohammed, come and look. Give me a theory, now."

Jenna's first thought was that the crew mistakenly arrived in the very ancient past or some other dimension. Not the future at all.

What if the calculations are wrong? Or, what if this is a separate dimension? A parallel world? No, MIND can't be wrong, it's impossible. Isn't it?

While questions fought for attention in her mind, Mohammed jumped up and placed the glasses over his eyes.

"I… I'm not…" was all he managed to say for almost a minute.

"Something's wrong here, Commander," he announced. "Gravity wouldn't allow for such large arachnids."

Jenna could only agree and if those creatures came near the capsule, what were they to do?

What would she do?

The last orders of the project's leader, Director Anthony Kust, rattled around in her mind, "If you encounter new life forms, hide, do not show hostility, no matter what the cost."

This order was given for a very valid reason.

Humankind, after its terrible and brutal Third World War, were now singular and in harmony with their goals for the first time in recorded history. The aim was to venture out into the universe and seek friendship, not war, never war again. Humanity had to find a way to rid themselves of their fear of anything different from their own selves and encourage compassion inside. Every life form was to be given respect and equality. It was the core message of the Global United space force.

A prime directive and one set in stone absolute.

"Get inside," Jenna said. "Now."

Kent was the first into the capsule, Mohammed collected his samples, and followed, mumbling about working in his small lab.

A bad feeling swirled around inside Jenna. Her stomach plummeted and twisted.

Where are we? When are we? This all makes no sense.

One last look through the glasses showed the group was coming closer. She entered the capsule and closed it firmly.

She felt her skin crawl with disgust at the thought of the eight-legged monstrosities and what was the horned creature?

There was nothing they could do except hide inside the large machine. It was not equipped for further flight after the initial launch or even equipped for maneuvers. She could only hope the group would show no interest or miss the sight of the capsule completely.

"Rechecking readings," Kent called.

She crossed the short walkway and back into her seat at the main control panel.

"And?" she asked.

"According to MIND, we're two thousand years into the future almost exactly to the hour we left," Kent verified. "And eight miles away from the location of our base."

"Can MIND be wrong, Kent?"

"No."

"What are these things?"

"Commander, two thousand years is a very long time. Anything could have happened to our species. Anything. Perhaps even something catastrophic."

That was exactly what Jenna was worried about.

"Call the EYES back," she ordered. The bad feeling inside her grew stronger.

Please God, don't let us be attacked.

Jenna prided herself on being fearless and yet her insides swirled with fright, apprehension, and the beginnings of frantic terror. Not just for herself, but for the two men by her side.

Stay calm. Rational. They'll walk past us. They won't see us. Please, God.

"Commander. Something isn't right here," Mohammed called. "I was in the lab and…"

"Not now," Jenna snapped. "Give me a visual on the group, MIND."

MIND arranged onboard cameras and focused. The group was running. Running and scurrying straight towards them.

They move like spiders too, oh my...

"Can they damage the capsule?" Kent asked. The question was needless. Of course they could, and they all knew it. Damage to sensors and onboard equipment might mean a death sentence for those inside. It would almost certainly mean no return trip.

"Commander, what do we do?" Kent gently spoke. The calmness in his voice soothed Jenna's racing heartbeat. She closed her eyes and recalled all her training. All those never-ending trials and simulations.

Breathe, think, breathe. I can handle this.

The group was close, running at full-on speed. They had many hours until the capsule would be able to return home.

We can just hide. Stay inside until they've gone. Can't we?

"We lay low," she said.

Kent did not look convinced.

Only minutes later, a fast blur raced past the screen and a shrill alarm began to sound. The EYES had returned. Jenna raced off to get all four back inside before the group would be upon them.

Quickly, she checked the small armory. One loaded pistol. For emergencies only.

This is an emergency!

Surely they had the right to defend themselves should the worse happen. It wouldn't be hostility or a fear of the unknown to defend, would it?

They had to get back, get home, with the data.

Again she watched the outside camera screen. The biggest creature, the one she saw first, had reached the capsule. The spiders were unleashed and crawling slowly.

Using its spear, the horned creature poked at the outer titanium shell twice.

Immediately, alarms sounded. Jenna silenced each one and waited.

"I thought they might choose to pass us by," she said. "We've no time to think."

"It has to be some kind of evolution, I mean. Or, genetically created, lab-made," Kent whispered. "It looks as if it has superior body mass and height. It's curious too."

"Why would evolution work backward?" Mohammed answered. "And it's too quick, isn't it? This doesn't make sense and the lab showed..."

"We don't know what's happened yet," Kent interrupted. "It could be a mutation or a new genetically designed species. Those arachnids might be mechanical. Advanced Artificial intelligence."

Jenna half-listened to the conversation and half-watched the screen. Something about the horned creature unsettled her deeply. Some kind of familiarity in the way it looked, moved, and walked. The four arachnids clustered behind it, before they began to circle the capsule, only stopping to tap on its sides.

"We need a plan, Commander," Kent said. "Sensors could be destroyed."

"I know, I'm thinking. I'm open to suggestions," Jenna answered.

"A warning shot," Kent said. "Fire a warning shot."

"The hostility pact. We can't," Mohammed cried. "It's a hostile act. They could attack. We should communicate with them! Or stay inside."

A heavy bang sounded.

'Warning, sensor sixty-seven offline,' MIND announced.

"Shit!" Jenna cried. "Warning shot it is."

There's no other choice. There isn't. I'm doing the right thing.

Quickly, she opened the armory and grabbed the pistol. She ran to the outer door, confident in her actions.

Communication would be far too difficult, if not impossible. Jenna knew that. Who the hell could communicate with giant spiders?

No, a warning shot would scare them away. It had to work; she was right.

After all, hadn't she navigated a shuttle through the sudden breakup of an asteroid? Yes.

Hadn't she landed an unstable ship on Mars, alone? Yes, she had, and she knew what she was doing.

She was going to scare the creatures, that's all. Frighten them away with a single shot before the capsule was ruined.

To cause fear in an unknown species was considered a hostile action, but she could explain it to her superiors. It was the right decision. They would understand.

"Commander," Mohammed called from behind her. "Please listen to me. This isn't the correct move."

Jenna ignored him and ordered MIND to open the outer door. She crouched to her knees and held the almost weightless gun firmly.

I can do this. I can do this.

As the door opened, the horned creature stood just ten feet away. Its yellow eyes and dark red fur, its horns, and strange cloven feet filled her vision. It looked almost like a tall goat standing on its hind legs.

Her eyes met the eyes of the creature. The two stared at one another.

Revulsion. Hate. Feelings of disgust rose inside Jenna. Emotions she couldn't fight.

A spark of something ancient lit. An awakening of primal fears and cellular knowledge. Ancestor memory.

Images bombarded her, memories of her childhood in a small religious community. Old stories of demons and devils, of Revelations and the end of days.

To her, the creature resembled paintings of devils, images straight from ancient books of world religions, straight from her own holy book.

It's going to attack. It's going to slaughter us.

The creature stepped back and raised its hairy arms. Jenna began to shake. One half of her mind told her the creature was surrendering. It was scared. It feared her. Yet, she feared it more. Unnaturally so.

Every atom of her body quivered with terror at the sight of the creature.

For her, it could only be a monster conjured from nightmares themselves. Alive in the future and risen from the pits of burning hell in a future Armageddon.

A spider appeared, legs crept over the side of a large boulder, slowly moving, creeping, threatening, ready to pounce.

The emotion of hatred swarmed around her mind. She had never witnessed anything so frightening, anything so different to herself. The look, the sense of it overcame her orders and rules, overcame her need for peace, for humanity's peace. Overcame her common sense.

The horned creature made a strange guttural sound and knelt, a further submission.

Jenna believed her very soul was being violated, just by being in its presence. Disgust and intolerance surfaced. Brutal, cold terror.

For her, the monster wasn't a natural creature. It was abhorrent. It was evil personified. It was Lucifer in flesh, or one of his disgraceful minions. She could feel its wrath and desire to destroy her. She knew what to do. She had no doubt.

Jenna fired the gun.

The creature fell back and lay still. The scene around her froze. None of the spiders moved one inch.

Hands pulled on her shoulders, dragged her inside. The door closed with a thud.

Chaos, shouts of fury, cries of disbelief.

"Why! Jenna! What have you done?!"

Jenna tried to say she couldn't help herself. It had to die. It was the epitome of evil after all. They all had to die. It wasn't natural. It was wrong, all wrong.

Cold shock flooded her. She found herself pulled to her seat and shaken by her shoulders.

"I'm relieving you of command!" Mohammed wailed.

Jenna could not answer. She only found herself gazing at the screen, gazing at the spiders moving, leaving, and disappearing around a rock face.

What was wrong with Mohammed? She'd saved them, she'd saved them all. Maybe even saved their souls. She sat and struggled to lower her heartbeat while the two men argued and bickered.

She took a deep breath and held her head in her hands.

I did the right thing. I did. The future is a literal Hell on Earth.

"They might be civilized, and she killed one!" Mohammed shouted. "Just because they looked different! Will we never learn! Something isn't right here; I'm telling you the insects are the same as our timeline. That's not…"

It was then that someone knocked on the outer door three times. Three sharp raps.

"What the…" the two men said in unison.

"MIND, who or what is outside?" Alex asked.

MIND decided not to reply. Three more knocks sounded, the awful noise of clanging metal.

"It's more of them, they've come to kill us," Jenna whispered. "I felt what they are. Pure evil. Can you feel it?"

No one spoke. Only stared, afraid of the unknown outside.

Three more knocks.

The ultimate deceivers, the fallen ones, in the future, they all rule. That's our future.

And now they've come to kill us. Armageddon happened. The end of days. Revelations. The beast. It's all true.

Three more knocks rang out.

MIND's screen burst with loud static and turned the color of blood. Two chilling, shock-inducing words flashed across, 'SIMU-LATION FAILURE.'

"I knew it," Mohammed spoke. "I just knew it."

The outer door opened and with long heavy strides. In walked their project leader, Anthony Kusk. He shook his head slowly from side to side, eyes full of disappointment.

How is he here?! This is impossible.

Jenna's mind buckled in confusion.

I don't understand...

She glanced at the computer screen once more. Failure.

Slowly, comprehension dawned. There was no time travel. They were not in the future at all.

She tried to stand, tried to speak, and salute. Tried to apologize and failed. It was all too much. Her brain jolted and did the kindest thing it could do for her: a temporary shutdown. For her, the world went black again.

Three weeks later

Jenna stood outside the G6 block. The staff building on the private Arizona base she had called her home for two years. By her feet stood a single suitcase.

She was leaving, and not of her own accord.

A psychological experiment was what they called her team's fake trip through time. Carried out with holographic technology, mechanical beings... and vicious cruelty too, as far as she was concerned.

The crew had only been launched a few miles to a remote area just miles from the base. One final test for the genuine journey that would soon be carried out.

Mohammed had been selected for the final team.

Jenna and Kent had not. Kent was still needed as part of the support team staying behind. Jenna was not.

Emptiness sat inside her, shame and embarrassment. For two days after the events, she hadn't been able to fully comprehend the simulation. She'd been overwhelmed, confused and for a week had laid in a hospital bed in shock.

She'd been so certain, so *sure* that they were in the future.

The creature was no more than clever make-up and a costume. Military personal, playing an acting role. The spiders, A.I. and remotely controlled. No one had been killed. The pistol she shot carried blanks. It was all a test, an illusion to see how they each could handle contact with the unknown and something which might personally invoke the fear response in the commanding officer.

For the first time in her life, Jenna had failed.

As the car pulled up to take her anywhere she longed to go, she stopped and took a moment to look at the stars, as she so often did.

She had been out there, to space and to Mars. She had traveled further than almost anyone she knew. For her, that hadn't ever been enough. But now it had to be.

She had no idea what life held for her, but clearly, time travel was not her fate.

She wondered if it should be anyone's fate.

The flight or fight reflex, the survival instinct to kill to save oneself or loved ones, was something she owned in spades. Something she believed all humans owned, along with fear of the unknown.

Certain traits, she believed, made a human *human*. Those traits stopped humanity from running headlong into dangerous situations without a single thought.

There was a reason humans fear arachnids, more than cellular memory. They could kill.

Fear was not something she wanted to overcome. It was something she believed everyone needed.

Hostility was not warmongering as far as she was concerned. Aggression wasn't always inherently negative. No, hostility *did* have a place. Hostility and fear could mean the difference between survival and death.

Of all the tests run on that same scenario, only one commander had chosen to communicate with the creatures. She would be leading the *real* exploration through time.

When the day arrived to actually send Mohammed and his new team far off into the future, and if they arrived at their *real* destination to find aggressive life forms… well, maybe then they would wish their commander was Jenna.

Until then, she would have all the time in the world…

Jenna Cartwright, age forty-three. Explorer, astronaut, brave, loyal, and not without fear.

Might there come a day when we, humanity, won't fear unknown life forms that look so different to us? Or will our first reaction always be one of hostility and fright?

Maybe somewhere, out there, in space or time, a race might find us terrifying to look at.

They might feel revulsion at our appearance, and they may have good reason to…

WILL THE REAL ALEXANDER PLEASE STAND UP

People are a product of their genetics and environment only.

People are much more than a product of genetics and environment.

What if?

Suspend your disbelief...

For your entertainment, meet Mr. Simon Obea and his new very wealthy client with an unusual problem...

Simon Obea made himself comfortable in his plush chair and stared at the immaculately dressed woman seated across from him.

She was elegant and draped with expensive jewellery. Simon guessed she had more wealth around her throat than he might earn in his lifetime.

Are those real diamonds? He thought. Yes, they must be!

Next, he wondered why a woman of her fame, wealth, and status might need a lawyer like himself. He was only used to defending criminals, the corrupt, and only had cases no one else wanted to touch.

Now, Ms. Kirsty Smyth sat in his office, her muscled security team outside. He knew who she was, everyone knew who she was, but what did she want with him?

That was the big question. He cleared his throat and smiled, made eye contact with her shrewd, calculated gaze.

"So, Ms. Smyth, I must admit I'm surprised to see you here. What is it you think I can do for you?"

"I want my son back," she stated. She leaned back and raised an eyebrow, as if daring him to ask further questions.

"Is there some mistake? I read online that you won custody of your son after the big custody battle. It made the news everywhere."

"No mistake. However, I said I want *my* son back and I expect you to help me achieve that."

"I understand," Simon said, even though he did not understand at all.

"Does your ex-husband have him?" He asked.

"In a sense, yes."

So he's been kidnapped? Shouldn't she be at the police station? The FBI?

"A kidnap?"

"Not at all Mr. Obea."

This is going to be a long day.

"Please, Ms. Smyth, perhaps you could explain further?"

"Very well. I assume our conversation is secure and confidential?"

"Yes, of course."

"There were aspects to our court case that remain sealed, classified if you will. You said you read online about the custody battle?"

"A little," Simon answered.

That was a lie. Like most people, he'd followed the case very closely. Such wealthy people under public scrutiny were always of interest.

He'd followed the divorce case too; everyone had been staggered by the eye-watering amount of money at stake and divided.

"We battled for a week, my ex-husband and I. For sole custody and then joint. I carried that boy in my own womb, Mr. Obea. I can assure you I fought hard, and I wouldn't agree. My ex-husband, Richard, is an obstinate man. He did, however, suggest an alternative solution. One that was kept out of the press."

"And that was?"

"Cloning. We had our boy cloned."

Holy shit!

"I... I... Wow."

"Indeed. Richard paid sixteen million dollars to a private, highly unregulated company for a copy of our son, right down to the very last detail. A clone was created and grown rapidly to be the same age, with absolutely no difference between it and the real boy. Alexander, my son, his consciousness was mapped by a quantum machine and downloaded, copied if you will. Memories, character traits, and so on… The clone was created for Richard. Not for me."

"This is… well, forgive me, but it's impossible!"

"I assure you it isn't. It exists, and it worked, Mr. Obea."

Simon gasped out loud. He had no idea such technology already existed. Of course, cloning techniques had been available some time, he knew that. His own neighbour had his dog cloned when the original passed away of old age. His own wife had suggested they do the same with their cat.

The advertisements were on the television all the time. But people, actual human beings, that was new to him.

"It was all very hush, hush, as you can imagine," Ms. Smyth continued. "After all, it really only is available to the elite of our society."

"At that cost, yes, I suppose it is," Simon agreed.

Sixteen million dollars!

"Hair and a blood sample, scans, questions, that's all it took. My husband, however, tricked me. A thing I don't find amusing in the slightest. I have the wrong one, Mr. Obea. I have the clone and I want *my real* son back. The one I carried in my womb, the one I raised. Not the one designed and created in a lab."

Simon's mind stepped into overdrive. How was such a thing even possible? Or, more importantly for him, how much would a case like hers earn him? Thousands or more, easily.

Simon wasn't concerned with the ethics of the case, the implications, or the sense of what was right or wrong. No, about those things, he cared not.

He sensed the case might be the first of its kind. It could make him famous and in high demand. He could move out of his one-bedroomed home into something larger and with a pool, a house his wife would love.

Simon blinked quickly and pulled his thoughts back. One thing above the others bothered him.

"Ms. Smyth, if in fact, these boys are absolute duplicates, clones. How will we prove who is the original? Surely they can't be the exact same?"

"I'll know. I can *tell*. A mother has a special sense. The thing I have in my possession is *not* my birth child."

The thing!

"Would it be possible to meet the… clone?"

"Yes, he's outside."

Simon's stomach lurched at the thought. He wanted, no, needed time to prepare. It was all far too sudden. He needed a plan.

Think of the money, the money!

"Wonderful," he found himself saying. "Let's bring him in."

Ms. Smyth did not move. Instead, she shouted for security.

Simon watched as his own office door burst open. A wide man with a gun on his hip filled the doorway.

"Fetch the boy," she ordered. The guard did as he was told and while Simon's own stomach filled with butterflies, a boy of eleven was gently pushed forward into the room.

The blonde-haired child looked utterly forlorn and desperately sad. His small head hung low, as if only the immaculately cleaned carpet could hold his interest.

Is there something wrong with him?

"Hello," Simon said. Despite himself and his greed, he couldn't help but feel pity and sympathy for the sad boy.

The only reply was a small nod of his head.

This is all too… strange. This is a clone. Wow.

"I'm Simon," Simon said. "And you are?"

"Alexander," the small boy replied.

"No, he isn't," Ms. Smyth interrupted. "He's the copy, the fake. They were swapped. I know it."

The boy's lower lip began to tremble. Simon felt his heart skip a beat in solidarity.

"Perhaps I could speak to your… Alexander alone," he dared to ask.

To his surprise, Ms. Smyth stood and left the room, her expression one of severe distaste, directed towards the child.

No sooner was the door shut than the boy fled to him and into the warm chair his mother vacated. Pleading blue eyes latched onto his own.

"Help me, please! I'm the real Alex and she doesn't believe me!"
Well shit. Simon thought. This is going to be a very long day.

***

"I remember everything. I remember when they took some of my hair and pricked my finger for blood. I remember falling off a swing when I was seven and cutting my lip. Look, I still have the scar."

Simon peered closely; the boy did indeed have a thin scar. "I know everything about myself because I'm me. But she's horrible to me now. She used to love me and we were so close and now she won't even look at me!"

The boy burst into tears. Simon rummaged in a drawer for tissues and gently passed one over.

This is over my head. What can I possibly do to fix this?! This isn't a case for a lawyer. How would a court even judge this?! Is Ms. Smyth delusional? Paranoid? Did neither parent see this coming?

He rubbed his temples and felt a headache start.

"You're quite sure you're the real one?" He asked.

"Yes," Alexander answered. "I am. I'm me! I've never seen the other one, he lives with my father. It's not fair, I didn't want to be cloned. I just wanted the arguments to stop, that was all. Father won't even see me, he doesn't need to because he's got me, another me!"

They paid sixteen million dollars for this. What a mess. What company did this!

"Let me think, kid," Simon said. "Just let me think for a minute."

If he wasn't the real one, would he still think he was? What can I do?

Simon had the beginnings of an idea. He could swap them. Swap the boys over. Without the father knowing too, was such a thing even possible?

Can I? Should I?

"Please help me," the boy pleaded.

Simon took a deep breath and shook his head. Shook away the dollar symbols he felt were etched on his eyeballs like an old cartoon.

"Where does your father live?" He asked.

"The other side of town, in the mansion district. Me and Mother live in the big estate she owns. But she wants me out. Gone."

"One more thing: do you know which company did this?"

"I don't know. I'm sorry. Father knew the judge, he paid people off and bribed them all. I don't know where we went."

But, if he remembers the tests, surely he must be the real one?

"If I suggest a plan," Simon said. "To fix this mess, will you go along with it?"

"Yes! Anything. I'll do anything."

Simon's reasoning was simple. To him. Smoke and mirrors. Plain old-fashioned deceit.

If both boys were clones, one created at the same age and with the same character traits and memories, then a person really wouldn't know the difference.

He believed Ms. Smyth's problem might be psychological in nature. He concluded that she must have persuaded herself that *her* Alexander was the wrong child.

Slowly, he stood and approached his office door.

I hope this works.

There she was, outside, composed and as regal as ever.

"A quick word?" Simon asked. She nodded and raised an eyebrow.

"I'll swap them," Simon whispered low so his receptionist or the security guards wouldn't hear. "I promise you I'll go now and I'll swap them over so your husband won't know a thing."

"No court case?"

"We can if you prefer. I thought it might be prudent to avoid more publicity. For one flat fee, I'll do this for you."

"Ah, and how much do you want?"

Say a million, say a million.

"Two million dollars."

"Done."

Simon Obea could not believe his luck.

***

An hour later, he found himself in his own car. The child, Alexander, sat at his side.

"We got two choices here, kid. One, I swap you, you live with your father. Two, we drive, get some lunch, take you back and we lie."

"Lie?"

"Yes, we pretend we swapped you."

"That's very deceitful, Mr. Obea. It's wrong."

"And cloning you wasn't?"

The child fell silent. The road was fairly quiet, with a small amount of traffic on one side, and a beautiful view of the beach and ocean on the other.

Alexander chose to stare at the cool water.

If he is the wrong one, would he even know he was?

Simon was not a philosophical man. He was no deep thinker. He enjoyed the law and loved making money above all things.

He concentrated on visualizing the huge amount of cash landing in his bank account.

"We'll lie," the boy abruptly said. "But first, I want to see him. I want to meet him. Please, and then I'll play along."

"Curiosity killed the cat," Simon warned.

"But satisfaction brought him back," Alexander answered with a small grin. Simon had to admit, the kid was a one-off, smart, and humorous too.

If I had a clone, would I want to meet him? Yes, I suppose I would. Maybe I should swap them anyway?

"Okay Kid, you got yourself a deal. Now, tell me where to go."

A little peek wouldn't hurt.

Huge security gates and a small hut containing guards prevented access to the mansion district. Simon immediately saw the problem, Alexander did not.

"I know them, they'll let me in," he promised. "Father's house is at the top of the hill."

Simon shrugged and drove forward. Immediately an armed guard popped up and held up one hand as a stop gesture.

Alexander opened the car window and waved.

"It's me, Alex. I forgot my pass again, sorry!"

"No problem," the man relaxed, grinned, and opened the gates. "Go on in."

Well, that was easy!

Simon drove until he parked outside a huge mansion. The house was a tall eccentric-looking building, with towers and a lush, expertly tended garden.

It must have twenty bedrooms at least. The size of it!

Simon was busy drooling at the building when the boy opened the car door and ran across the lawn.

Shit!

"Hey! Come back."

For Simon, Alexander was two million dollars running away. He scrambled out of the car and raced after him.

He found the boy half-hidden behind a bush, gazing into one of the main windows. A child exactly the same as him sat in a large chair reading a book. Close by, a man worked on a holographic laptop screen.

He bent over breathless and gasped, sweat poured down his spine.

"Kid, we need to go. You've had your look, okay? We'll be seen, caught, and then it's over."

"He took my life, Mr.Obea. That boy, he's taken my life."

"Then we'll…"

Alexander raised his arm and rapped on the glass sharply.

"Shit!" Simon cried.

Now what! Now what do I do?

His stomach sank all the way to the floor. Surely it meant his fee, all that money, was gone.

***

Simon found he was too uncomfortable to form any words.

On a plush sofa facing him, both versions of Alexander sat staring at one another in wonder.

Alexander's father, Richard, paced the expensively decorated room.

"I knew she'd do something like this, I knew it," he mumbled. "She took half my money, half my estate and now she wants my boy."

Simon opened his mouth and closed it again. He'd expected to be thrown out of the mansion estate. Instead, the two had been invited, no, pulled inside swiftly.

"How much did she offer to pay you for this?" Richard asked Simon.

"Three million dollars," he lied.

"I'll triple it. I'll triple your fee if you lie. We agreed on cloning because *she* was supposed to be moving to Europe. They were never meant to meet. I didn't think she'd realize she had the copy."

Nine million dollars! Nine million dollars all for me! Wait what? He is the copy!

"She is going, as soon as she has the real me," both boys said in absolute unison. Not even a single vowel was out of sync.

With a jolt of horror, Simon realized he had no idea of which boy was which any longer.

Both wore virtually the same clothing, the same sneakers, the exact same expressions. Mannerisms appeared to be the same, the boys even blinked at the same time.

"Which one of you came with me?" Simon asked. "Why are you wearing the same clothes?"

Both boys raised a hand and spoke in unison, "Because we're the same. Same houses, same clothes."

No, you've got to be kidding me! Shit, shit, shit! Now what?

Simon felt as if he had fallen very deeply down a hole he might never be able to climb out of.

"Huh?" he said.

"Alexander lived with both myself and my wife. Two sets of clothing etc. Custody was shared until *she* decided on a move to Europe. That's what started this mess," Richard said. "Now, which one of you is the copy?"

Neither boy spoke.

If this all goes to hell, that woman will ruin me.

"Stop fooling," Richard cried. "Alex," he said, and pointed to the boy on the left. "Come and stand here. Now, Mr. Obea, I will write you a guaranteed cheque. You will take that boy and tell my ex-wife they've been swapped. Do you understand me?"

Simon did. He understood very well, and he wanted nothing more than to leave the situation.

That makes eleven million dollars! Which boy did I bring? Who cares!

A bubble of excitement rose inside his chest. He hiccupped loudly.

"Of course," he managed to agree. "Of course I will."

***

"So, which one are you really?" Simon asked.

He was floating on air and driving again, driving to Ms. Smyth's private estate with Alexander by his side. But which Alexander?

Does it matter? As long as she's fooled.

Simon began to laugh out loud. The events of the day felt like a wild comedy.

When he'd woken up that same morning, he'd had no idea of what an unusual day it would turn out to be. He couldn't wait to tell his wife.

"I'm the real Alexander," Alexander said.

"Yes, you are," Simon laughed. "And that's what you'll tell your mother."

As he drove, the implications of his sudden huge wealth kicked in. Simon had grown up in the poor district. Through sheer force of will, he had managed to escape and attend university on a scholarship, gaining a law degree. He was always scraping by, always trying to make ends meet. He understood that money, the thing that had plagued him his whole life, would never be a worry of his again.

By the time the two pulled up and Ms. Smyth's private estate, he was still grinning.

The reunion was a sweet one. Ms. Smyth's cold barriers came crumbling down at the sight of her son. She sobbed and held him tightly.

I'm sure he's the same one she had. Or is he? Though Simon had no clue, he was at least glad to witness such happiness.

Maybe Richard panicked and made the error?

Briefly, he went inside while Ms. Smyth wrote him a cheque. "We'll be going to Europe soon. Thank you, Mr. Obea. For everything."

Alexander winked once behind her back. That was enough for Simon, enough to tell him.

All the same, he pocketed his cheque and left. Left the madness behind and drove straight to the bank before it closed.

He was going to go home and take his wife out to the most expensive restaurant he could find. He was going to tell her he was retiring and tell her she could quit her tough and demanding job. He was going to tell her she could have everything she ever wanted, although cloning the cat would be off the list.

Simon laughed all the way to the bank.

***

Richard Smyth walked into the lawyer's office and sank into a tall leather chair.

"How can I help you, Mr.Smyth?" The lawyer, Mr. Connolly, asked with eyes full of greed. He knew who the man was, everyone knew. He was beyond wealthy and highly influential.

"I want my son back," he said. "My ex-wife has him, she's in Europe. I have the wrong one, you see. I was tricked."

"I'm not sure I follow," Mr. Connolly said.

Richard sighed loudly and began to explain…

Nurture or nature, cellular, genetic memory.

Souls. Is a personality ingrained and set or pliable? Can consciousness be copied and downloaded?

Mirror images. Flawless.

Could you tell yourself apart from yourself? What if you were the clone?

Might the answers be found somewhere in the future? Somewhere in the realm between truth and fact. Between comprehension and incomprehension…

THE KEEPER OF THE LAKE

Meet Ella, a lonely, friendless young woman who feels most out of place on dry land.

Occupation- None. School attendee.

Destination-Beneath the surface.

Can a friendship be formed between two very different life forms?

Can an unbreakable bond exist between a human and the unknown?

Maybe somewhere in the middle ground between light and shadow...

In the seconds it took for Ella's body to hit the water, a sense of wholeness existed inside her. She entered a universe that was something of her own. The lake never repelled her; the surface never pushed her away like people often did. The water never felt repulsed by her. Only welcoming, it lured and pulled. Invited her to dwell within the sharp coolness underneath.

The water, Ella believed, was her true home. She dived into the lake with a graceful and elegant arch. She hit the surface with barely a splash and plummeted still into her own secret world of wonder.

Sixteen-year-old Ella swam daily, regardless of the weather. A deep need, a craving for her addiction, twisted inside her like a swarm of bees if she ever had to miss a single day.

At age five, Ella could hold her breath a full minute longer than her own strong lunged mother.

"That girl was born with gills!" Her father would say. "She's a fish-girl!" her mother would tease. Ella and her invisible gills became a long-running family joke.

Her true passion for water, lakes, and oceans, wild seas, and intricate city canals had started at age eleven. Her thirst for knowledge of the lifeforms beneath the surface kicked in soon after. When Ella wasn't in the nearby lake, at school, or asleep in her narrow bed, she would watch the calm surface of the water, barely content with only being close. She longed for the world beneath the glorious shimmery surface.

Some people say that life has two paths and that the action of turning either left or right can determine a person's entire fate. For Ella, those choices were above or below. She always chose the below. The world above held pain for her. At school, she was bullied, a target for those that considered her quiet nature to be far too different. Ella, with her elfin features, quietness, and mysterious ways. At home, her parent's arguments over their lack of money could be heard raging day and night.

Only water held freedom for her, peace. A chance to breathe in the one place she couldn't.

Ella swam and held her breath effortlessly.

She whirled among the many varied aquatic plants as the hot sun shone calmly on the surface above her. She loved the jagged effect the sunlight gave.

The color was simple below, lush greens and browns, but for her, the design was more vibrant and alive than the colors of the world above.

She felt the burn in her lungs and knew she was close to her limit; she swam upwards with the forceful kicking towards necessary air.

She broke the surface with a flourish. A multitude of sounds immediately hit her senses. A greedy seagull, busy and scouting for food, the low purr of a speedboat somewhere far off. Laughter, high-pitched, with squeals of pretend fright. Ella turned.

The raft! Of course, she thought.

The old wooden platform bobbed on the surface, held up by old, rusty oil drums. Chained down and anchored below. Ella had gripped the chain many times and followed its thick length up and down. It was the place she practiced holding her breath and two minutes, fifteen seconds was her best record.

Another high-pitched squeal erupted along with the sound of a deep male voice laughing close behind it. Ella turned just as an empty beer can bounced painfully off her skull.

"Bullseye!" One of the girls shouted while the rest jeered.

Ella's stomach sank. It was her classmates from school, the ones that hated her, though she had no idea why. She had tried to fit in and failed. Once she had decided to be her true self, the bullying began.

She liked to keep to herself. She liked to learn everything she could so she could leave with good grades, gain a scholarship, and study the secrets of the oceans themselves.

"Throw a full one!" another girl shouted. "It's that ugly freak," yelled another.

Ella dived. Back into her own place, back into her home. She swam and passed a group of frantic little fish who paid her no attention. She passed more plants who chose to sway towards her as if they were strands of hair in the wind, calling her.

She touched the coarse sand and stopped to enjoy the gritty feel on her fingertips. She pushed forward to the shore. As her lungs began to burn once more, a glow caught her eye. Through the haze of the water, Ella saw a blur of sharp movement. She stilled for a moment and found herself rising. She dashed up and into the air. She took a few deep breaths and dove down again.

What the… What is that?

A pale translucent figure hovered above the sand, half-hidden among curling seaweed. It emitted a slight glow, a shine almost. Ella watched in confusion as she longed for breath. Up to breathe, then back down again. Whatever it was, was gone. Vanished in the few seconds she took for air.

Frustrated, she left the water, determined to study her books on marine life later, and sat on the shore. *Maybe it was just my eyes? My imagination? Lack of air? A trick of the light?*

She watched the calm water and enjoyed seeing the birds swooping down. She enjoyed the summer months the most. She loved the lake in all weather, although she was banned from swimming when it froze in winter. It was deemed too dangerous by her mother.

Her heart sank as she focused her eyes on the group from school. She hoped the raft wouldn't become their regular hangout place. For Ella, the lake was hers.

***

The next day was Sunday. The one day she could swim twice. Morning and afternoon. Hardly anyone was around as Ella ran into the lake at eight in the morning, half-asleep and weary. The moment she hit the water she came alive. Truly alive. A jolt of electricity poured through her as she stretched and twirled, an underwater dance of her own making. Every two minutes, she would break the surface briefly and plummet down, disappearing under again.

On her fourth dive, she saw the glowing figure.

The previous night, she had flipped through every library book she had on marine biology. Nothing had come close to what she had seen. Shyly, without confidence, she had told her parents.

"It's your imagination," her mother said. "Didn't you stay up and watch that *Creature of the Lagoon* film the other night?"

"Creature of the Black Lagoon, yes," Ella corrected.

"Well, it just fired up your imagination is all. I'll bet that's it."

"But what if it's something new? An undiscovered life form?" Ella asked.

"Don't be silly dear," her father laughed in that patronizing way he was prone to.

The subject was closed.

As Ella watched the shape, she witnessed the impossible. The glowing figure formed itself into a hazy sphere, an orb of blue pulsing, rippling light. It sped towards her faster than she could believe. Her eyes widened as shock burst through her. The glowing orb hit her gently in the stomach, a tiny push, and shot away.

Bubbles exploded from her mouth as she swam to the surface. Feeling fear for the first time in the lake, she swam to the shore. She climbed out, limbs aching and rubbery.

That was not my imagination! This has to be some kind of new lifeform! What should I do? Nobody will believe me! What is it?! Question after question tumbled over each other in her mind as she sat breathless and shaken.

Can I go back in? Is it safe? What if it isn't safe anymore? What will I do?

A sob of panic escaped her lips. The lake was the only place she ever felt safe, the only place she felt she could be her natural self.

Just try.

Carefully, she padded across the shoreline and back in, step by step. A calmness overcame her, a pull. Unable to resist her curiosity, Ella dived in.

Whatever it is won't hurt me. I'm fine. If it was dangerous, then I'd be hurt already, hurt or worse.

She swam across the surface until she got to the raft. She hauled herself up for a moment and gazed around. The lake stretched for as far as she could see. At the very end, it twisted and curved, thinned out until it met with the ocean. She wondered if something new, some rare lifeform, had ventured into her lake. She decided she would make a study, her first research project.

Filled with excitement, she plunged back into her domain.

She followed the thick chain to the ancient barnacle-covered anchor beneath, all the time counting seconds. She spun and pushed off the thick, soft sand and up. She glanced around as she began her climb.

She stopped and almost screamed as a jellyfish swam by. Impossible! Her mind screamed. There are no jellyfish in here! I've never seen a picture that looks like this one before!

The jellyfish began to pulse with light, dim at first. It picked up speed until it flashed pure white. Ella watched in horrified fascination.

Her lungs screamed as she broke the surface, coughing and spluttering. Blobs of white filled her vision as she waited for her eyes to adjust. A slight tickle on her feet made her yelp in surprise. She placed her face into the water and opened her eyes. The jellyfish danced around her feet playfully.

With a deep breath, Ella went under and dared to hold out her arm. She touched the jellyfish and felt a ripple of warmth spread through her. Excitement built inside.

Am I really doing this? It can't be dangerous? Can it?

The jellyfish wrapped itself around her leg, very gently, she stroked it. She smiled and swallowed a mouthful of water. Choking, she rose for air.

Then back down again.

The jellyfish had become an octopus.

I'm mad. That's what happened. I've gone mad, Ella told herself. I'm hallucinating or its lack of air.

In wonder, she held out her arm again. Tentacles embraced her into a hug. With a surge of sudden bliss and happiness, Ella hugged the octopus back. A feeling of love and joy burst across her chest.

Abruptly, it pulled away and vanished.

Ella returned to the raft and waited. Minutes passed, then an hour. Nothing. She jumped back in and swam to the shore, looking for her new friend on the way. On the shore, she waited still. Until her stomach rumbled hungrily. She left to go home, determined to return later.

She knew she had encountered something extraordinary, something that might also make her life wonderful.

***

The afternoon felt much hotter than the morning. The sun shone down in its hazy glare, spreading its warmth for everyone to enjoy.

Ella watched. Most of the town had come to visit the lake. Some were on boats, some sat on the soft sand, some sailed, some paddled and splashed. The raft was full of the kids from school, shouting, laughing, and drinking beer.

One world above, one world beneath, both so vastly different.

Ella padded across the golden sand and waded up to her knees. She stopped for a moment, paused so she could enjoy the journey from one world into another. She waded further in and under.

Down into the abyss of her paradise. Joy and bliss filled her as she twisted and turned. The water itself seemed darker, torn up, and murkier. Ella looked for her friend but found she couldn't see clearly. She rose for breath and headed for the shimmering sunlight above.

"The seal-girl came up for air!" One of the girls on the raft shouted. "Throw something," she ordered the others.

Ella dove again before anything could hit her. She grabbed the raft chain and followed it.

Why won't they ever leave me alone? At school, and now here too. Why won't they just stop? I never bother anyone.

The familiar pain in her lungs propelled her back up for air. She flipped in a graceful movement and headed up. Just before she broke the surface, Ella spotted a pulsing light beneath. She took a few steadying gasps of breath and rubbed her stinging eyes. A beach ball hit her and bounced off her shoulder.

She dived under.

The pulsing creature joined her; Ella felt a jolt of apprehension. In the hours she'd been home, the octopus had grown into a massive size, twice the size of her at least. The light inside it had its own hypnotic rhythm. A multitude of colors switched back and forth. Red, green, lilac, purple, blue. A flash of white blinded her.

Tentacles wrapped around her body, they caressed and stroked. Warmth engulfed her, she found comfort in the unknown touch. The fear she felt left her, a deep happiness replaced it. Instinctively, she knew the strange life form wouldn't hurt her. She also believed it knew she wouldn't hurt it.

Briefly, she closed her eyes and tried to record the feeling of joy in her mind. When she opened her eyes, the octopus creature she held had become a giant red squid.

An eye as big as her own head watched her curiously.

A bubble escaped her mouth. The squid mimicked her. She sped for the surface; the squid chased.

NO! She thought. It can't! What if someone sees?!

Ella felt more kinship for the unknown creature than anyone in her surface world. The desire to protect filled her.

Frantically, she tried to wave her arms, a warning to stop. The squid copied her; tentacles waved in the soft currents.

Ella broke the surface to tread water. She tried to figure out where in the lake she was.

"Go somewhere else, freak! Last warning."

She spun around; the raft sat meters from her face. It bobbed along casually as the group of four mocked her.

"Please, no... just stop," she gasped.

A full beer can hit her sharply in the face. Ella cried out in shock and pain as her nose started to bleed.

A huge tentacle with suction pads as big as dinner plates shot out of the water and whipped. Two of the four teens were knocked screaming into the deep.

Ella yelped and sank. Her friend, the strange creature, held two of her classmates from the raft in its tight grip. Their arms and legs flailed and kicked, their faces horrified and frightened. Thick lines of bubbles left their mouths as the creature held on. Ella thought she heard a scream of desperation as she froze, unsure of what to do. Quickly, she swam to the surface to warn the others.

An explosion of movement came from her right as a third person jumped in to save the others. A tentacle grabbed him, pulled, and yanked with vicious determination. Straight down, lower and lower, until Ella lost track. The water turned red around her.

Bits of flesh and hair floated past. Ella swam for breath. She gasped deeply and waved her arms. No one noticed her, no one ever did. She swam to the raft where a girl alone peered wide-eyed over the edge.

"Get back!" Ella coughed.

"What did you do, freak?!" she screamed. "Where are they?!"

What?! What did I do?!

"Get help!" The girl yelled. Her sunburnt face turned pale.

Ella whipped around; her eyes searched for a boat to wave down. She stopped.

I can't. No, No I won't. They'll kill it. Of course, they'll kill it. I can't let that happen.

Ella knew that if the town folk knew what she knew, they'd hunt the creature down and destroy it. Dissect it, study it, and do all kinds of terrible things. They'd never understand anything so different. They all wanted to claim the oceans and seas for themselves as well as the lands.

Tears stung her eyes as she waited.

"I'm sorry," Ella said. "I'm so sorry."

A thick tentacle appeared quietly behind the girl. It worked its way carefully towards her as if it had a life of its own and struck. The girl's scream was deafening and unnoticed.

Ella sank slowly beneath the surface. She watched as the tentacle squeezed the girl until there was a slow, almost calm explosion of blood.

If its nature is to kill, why am I alive? Where did it even come from? Why am I not scared of it?

The massive squid danced its way over towards her. Tentacles that seconds before killed, calmed, and stilled as they entwined themselves around her.

I'll protect you, Ella decided. I promise I'll protect you. Was it protecting me?

Her arms wrapped around its rubbery flesh as she soothed and stroked.

***

The next few days passed slowly for Ella, torturously so. She had been prohibited from entering the water because of her missing classmates. Still, she sat on the shore and anxiously hoped the creature would at least sense her nearness.

Divers, with specialist equipment, searched the lake. No traces of the missing four were found.

As soon as the sheriff announced the lake could be used again, Ella ran.

Without any hesitation, she jumped into the water and down. She looked, waited, and searched for two hours, only stopping for air.

Where are you? Her mind chanted. Please, please be here!

Exhausted, she hauled herself onto the stained raft and burst into tears.

It's gone! I didn't even get to say goodbye.

Pain tore through her as she felt overwhelmed by sadness. She felt as if she had lost the single most important thing in her life.

Her chest ached with hurt, despair, and loss.

A slight tickle on her foot made her gasp with hope. A light, a single pulsing light, shone dimly. Ella's heart leaped with joy as she jumped back in.

The creature was a sphere again, a small, beautiful lilac orb. Ella knew, she sensed her friend no matter what it made itself appear to be. The two embraced. She felt engulfed by wholeness, bliss, and wonder. Finally, she settled on love.

The orb dazzled her with a light show of its own. It settled on red before it dashed off playfully. Ella chased, only breaking for air. The two played together, a secret game of their own design. For the first time in her life, Ella felt the clarity of pure happiness.

I won't ever leave you. I promise, her mind made a pact. I'll always be here for you. I'll keep you a secret, I swear.

The strange red orb flashed white in reply.

She flipped over in an underwater somersault. The orb zoomed around her.

Ella swam up and broke the surface. She breathed in lungfuls of air and then back down. The orb grew as she watched. It flashed green and darted away. Ella chased, delighted and happy, certain she was in the world she truly belonged.

Many years passed, and Ella never left her small town. She became well known locally as the eccentric, happy, mysterious woman who swam in the lake every chance she had, no matter what the weather happened to be. She never missed a day. In the cold bitterness of winter, she would pace the shoreline, anxious to be back in her water.

Locals came to refer to her as '*The keeper of the lake.*'

Ella liked her nickname very much. She kept a study of her friend, one she never revealed or shared. A true lake keeper and also a true keeper of strange and wonderful secrets.

True friends are never apart, maybe in distance but never in heart, or so the saying goes.

Ella needed someone or something to be there for her. Not to fix her problems, or to offer advice, but to simply be there.

Friendship comes in many guises. Sometimes, from the unknown depths of the ocean and wild seas.

Ella found friendship with the unknown and rather than be fearful, she welcomed such a gift.

A life form originating from who knows where? A bond was made between the two and cherished.

A deadly bond, one-half of the two, killed to protect...

END NOTES

Interpretations are wildly different and many varied, as are opinions.

Still, I hope you have enjoyed these stories.

I don't get caught up with the mechanics of a tale, writing rules, and so on…

I tried many methods in the past, and it all felt wrong.

Right or not, I listen to my instinct because sometimes, that's all a person has.

I can only be me; I can only write as me and I refuse to be any different.

That feeling doesn't come from arrogance or stubbornness, but rather from an acceptance of self.

I like who I am, I like how I write, and I like that I do not fear being me anymore.

The way we each see the world is fascinating. I love how so varied we are in beliefs and outlooks, our skills, and our character traits.

Many of us are riddled with self-doubt. It is the enemy of a writer, especially when elitist attitudes exist.

The publishing world is now for everyone. We all like different things and styles. I adore that aspect.

Although, a few sleepless nights occurred putting this collection together. The same questions of *Is it good enough?* and *Am I good enough?* plagued me.

In the end, and for two reasons, I decided to do it anyway.

I write and publish because it brings me joy.

I write for fun.

For me, it really is that simple.

However, I truly hope all or some of these stories were fun for any reader.

Hopefully, a person might wonder what if, or they might laugh or smile.

And if not, then I hope I at least helped to provide a little escapism…

Much love,
Sarah Jane